# AL MORENO RIFT RESOLVER

## AND THE SOLUTION FOR THEAR

Mason J. Schneider

**Note:** This is a work of fiction. All of the characters and events portrayed in this book are fictitious and any resemblance to real people or events is purely coincidental.

Al Moreno Rift Resolver And the Solution for Thear

Cover art by MiblArt

www.riftresolver.com

ISBN: 9781650880563

# Other Works
# By Mason J. Schneider

## Al Moreno Rift Resolver Series:

The Crystal of Gosia – Book One

## The Wizard of the Night Series:

Wizarded Away – Book One

# Contents

# Regarding the Footnotes in this Book and a Word of Warning to Hardcore Sci-Fi Fans:

Yes there are footnotes. No, you don't *have* to read them. Yes, I think reading them makes the book better.

Now, it should be noted that this is a tale more closely aligned with the pulp-fiction days of old. Although it is set in the future and references advanced technology, the actual science behind some of these things may seem lacking to you. That being said, the focus is centered on the characters and their trial-some adventures of heroism. I hope you enjoy!

**- Mason J. Schneider**

In Loving Memory Of
Diamond

# PROLOGUE

"Erebus… we mustn't. He's only a babe."

"I've told you time and again sister love, Chaos have greater need of him than us. Think not for a moment I won't miss him too. I am the boy's father after all."

"It's not fair. Why should we have to give up a child when there are others… It is not *fair!*" she screamed the last word, her anger darkening the very night around them until it seemed even the stars hid for fear of her wrath.

"And 'twould be fair for another to give up their own? Besides my dearest Nyx, ours was chosen. We should be brimming with pride, *chosen* by Father himself! We are fortunate to have so many children, when some of the others you speak of have only one or none at all."

Her anger had momentarily subsided and a few brave stars had begun to peek out from their curtain of night. Now there was only understanding- sad, grief-ridden, painstaking understanding. She would have to give her newborn up. As she cradled him against her chest, her husband's arm around her, she pondered what life might be like for her son.

He'd never know her as his mother, never know how much it hurt her to give him away. All because Chaos demanded it. Despite the reason in her husband's words, it would never be fair to her. She knew not what the Universe[1] had in store for the babe. For all her power she still was not ever-seeing. No, he'd never know her, his siblings, nor his father- but he wouldn't be without them. She would guide him through every night. His father would lead him through any darkness. His siblings, well not all of them may sit well with the idea that he was chosen where they were not, but some of them would surely lend him compassion. She *hoped* anyway. And she did not hope for things often.

"'Tis time, sister." Erebus' announced. His black eyes never left the child.

And so, gathering up a bit of that strength that made her such a mighty goddess, Nyx cut her tears short. A single drop splashed from her eyes onto the babe at her chest. The only gift she dared to give him, for fear that there would be repercussions if Chaos

---

[1] Chaos, Universe = Same Guy

saw her give any more. And he saw *everything*, sure and true. A tear from the goddess of the night; it would surely make the boy fearless in whatever dark paths he may find himself journeying through life.

"Come children, say goodbye to your brother." Nyx smiled, a smile in place only to hide her pain from the little ones.

Not all of them appeared, some were busy with their own affairs. A few simply didn't show because they cared nothing for the boy; he was to be sent below anyway. Many of them stood around the edge of the dark balcony, watching their brother's goodbye from afar. But two of their children came closer to bid the babe farewell. First came a daughter of the goddess of night and god of darkness.

"He will suffer with them down there. Humans especially, they bring only misery to those around them. May death be swift when it comes to you little brother, a shame we didn't get to know each other." spoke Oizys.

Suddenly another daughter appeared beside the first. Quickly coming to her brother's defense, Philotes scowled at her sister as she spoke.

"You should not speak so drastically sister. Though you dwell in misery and suffering, and much of this our babe brother may witness beneath the heavens, he will see good in the worlds as well. When faced with misery there will be comfort for him in the friends I guide him to. Where there is suffering, he will find shortly after the satisfaction of triumph, despite it. You would be wise to look out for him with me, you never know when there'll be a time in which you need the boy's assistance."

Oizys scoffed, as if the idea of her needing help from one sent below the heavens was ridiculous. But she kept her mouth closed, looked once more at the newborn, then disappeared.

"Thank you for your kind words daughter, and for the vow to watch over him." Erebus looked fondly at Philotes as he expressed his gratitude.

Though he and his sister wife[2] had borne many children into existence, it seemed most of their personalities were centered around his epitome of darkness. Thus he was quite proud to have a daughter like Philotes, who seemed to be able to find good even in the worst of situations. She nodded respectfully to her father, smiled warmly at her mother, and kissed the babe gently on his brow before fading away.

---

[2] So the whole sister/wife husband/brother thing might be throwing you off- this derives from Greek mythology. Often times gods and goddesses with the same parents ended up having lots of little god children together. So yeah, it's as weird as it sounds but I wanted to keep the mythology in here as close to accurate as possible. You'll get over it :)

Next came an unexpected visitor, a goddess by the name of Gaea. She arrived clad in earth-green robes. She walked with a mighty step and both Nyx and Erebus looked up in surprise when the ground beneath them shook slightly as she came closer.

Nyx frowned, not overly fond of the goddess making an appearance at an event meant only for their immediate family. Once she had thought of her as a sister, but that was long ago when they were first born from Chaos. As much as she hated to admit it, the goddess *was* beautiful. Beauty in a pure, good-natured form, a kind that the goddess of the night had never known. And she certainly didn't want her husband getting any ideas. Before she could make a rude remark, however, Erebus spoke.

"We did not expect to see you here, Gaea. What is it that brings you to our domain, on the eve we bid our newborn babe farewell?"

"Slick back your hackles Nyx, I have no desire to bed with your brother of darkness. I've never really been one for the bad boy type." she laughed for a moment to herself before continuing, "I come with a proposal for the two of you."

The goddess of night narrowed her eyes in suspicion but nonetheless asked, "And what is the nature of this proposal?"

"Well it's certainly nothing to do with marriage. Worry not dear Nyx, my intentions today are pure. I have spoken recently to the Moirai[3] and they inform me of a great peril I will face in the years to come. They say there is only one who can save me from destruction, the very babe you hold in your arms. Thus my offer is simple, if this little one does indeed save me one day- I shall gift him passage back to the heavens so you may see him once more."

"We know little of his destiny, save that he was chosen by Chaos himself to leave us and serve the Universe from below. But if what you say turns out to be true, we would be grateful if you returned our son to us. Now if you don't mind, we must deliver the child to Father and 'twould be best if such a sensitive matter were done in private."

At Erebus' words Gaea gave a knowing smile and strolled away until she disappeared into the darkness around them. The other children of Nyx who had been watching from afar also faded away. And so now it was only the mother, father and son. The couple walked quietly to the edge of their dark domain and peered down below in silence for a moment.

---

[3] Also known as "The Fates", they know much of destiny and may be the fatherless daughters of Nyx herself. But let's keep that on the downlow for now, wouldn't want to get Erebus all worked up.

Below the edge of darkness could be seen a billion worlds, more stars than fathomable by our human minds, and the beautiful light they reflected across the gaps of empty space between them. For just a moment the thought flashed in Nyx' mind- she could hide the child. Perhaps if she said one of his brethren had killed him Chaos would pay them no mind and leave them as a family. But no, Father saw everything, sure and true. And before another treacherous thought could come to her mind, a split in the darkness opened up before them in a brilliant flash of purple. Chaos had arrived. It was time.

"Father, we have brought the child as promised." Erebus spoke to the rippling purple swirl of color that shone so brightly against the blackness all around them.

"Yes, you've brought the child, though it was not without struggle. I saw the devious thoughts in your wife's mind, the thoughts of betrayal that flashed within her. You were wise, daughter, to not listen to them. To go against me is to go against your very self."

Nyx dare not let her temper show and only muttered, "Apologies Father."

"Shall we be allowed to know his name, Great One?" Erebus asked, gazing into the swirling depths of the Universe itself.

"He shan't know his true name, but I suppose since the two of you have been good on your sacrifice you may be enlightened. Behold Lýsi, this newborn god I send below. Shall his destiny be fulfilled and his servitude to me, the All-Knowing, be fruitful for us all. The time is now. Hesitate not, Nyx and Erebus."

And so, not wanting any more of their Father's disfavor, Erebus took the infant from his wife and threw him into the swirling vortex that was Chaos itself. Down, down, down the babe went. As ignorant as any baby about what was going on, the poor thing had no idea the pain he was about to endure. At first it was soothing, the purple light swirling around him, like a warm tunnel that felt like home. And then excruciating pain. A pain that would have caused the strongest of mortals to cry out for their mothers. But alas, this was no mortal, this was a god. Son of the goddess of the night and the god of darkness themselves.

This pain had a purpose at least, as not all pain does. It was the process of binding the flesh of body to a soul that had never known one before. Lucky it was that he was only a child and had not yet grown used to being a soul in the heavens. For if an older god were to go through this same process, he'd surely cry out for his mother as well. It would feel like having been free one's entire life, then being forced into the tiny cage that is the human body. But he was only a babe, born not long ago[4]. And his own cries fell on empty ears, with only Chaos to hear the wailing. But at last it was done, the pain already forgotten. The soul of Lýsi bound to a human body. And out of the swirling purple tunnel he fell. Down, down, down.

And where did this newborn god, now encased in human form land? Why a roller-rink parking lot of course. Found off an exit of an incredibly busy intergalactic highway. Destiny has humorous beginnings indeed.

---

[4] "Not long ago" is a bit different in god-time. In human terms he would have been a little over five hundred or so years old.

# CHAPTER ONE

"Aaron, in the name of the gods and all things both holy and evil, *please* stop making that noise."

"What noise?" an innocent Aaron Flux asked, "Oh you mean the *Zoooop-toop-toop-toop*?"

"What else would she mean Flux?" Al glanced sidelong at the resolver.

"Aw c'mon man! Those baby Zamwoths on Jared[5] were so cute, they kept looking down on me with those fourteen big eyes and going *Zoop-toop-to-*"

Aaron was abruptly cut off by a smack across the back of the head from Marcie. He tenderly rubbed the

---

[5] The planet where Alfred, Aaron, Marcie and Henry just completed their most recent mission. Located in Sector Nine of the Quarrymith Galaxy, it is the native planet of only a single intelligent species- the Zamwoths. And while I'd love to describe to you the characteristics of one, I'm afraid it's quite pointless and has no relevance whatsoever to the story. Oh alright, if you insist…

The Zamwoth is a peaceful creature by nature, though one wouldn't guess so by their appearance. Males stand about fourteen feet tall and females have been recorded at upwards of sixteen. Equipped with six limbs; four are used for walking, a single "arm" protruding from the chest is used for various tasks such as eating, grabbing, etc. And the last limb is used for… well use your imagination.

spot with his hand, feigning much more pain than was likely caused.

"Yes, the creatures were very cute. Until they spit hallucinogenic paste on your forehead and you tripped balls the rest of the mission." Alfred laughed.

"Yeah I think that paste might still be working a little magic on me at the moment. Is there or is there not a dancing emu over there?" Flux pointed to the far corner of the ship and began swaying in some rough excuse of a rhythm.

"Alright, I know you don't like needles buddy but this has to stop. I'm injecting you with the sedative so you can sleep this off."

Aaron seemed not to hear or notice Al approaching him with the shot at all. As the needle slid into the vein at his wrist, his swaying gradually slowed until he slumped down in his chair. Alfred grabbed another chair and hoisted his friend's legs up to form a makeshift bed.

As Flux's eyes began to close he mumbled, "Hehe the emu said I'm his special frie-" and then he passed out.

"Thank the stars that's over with. I didn't know how much more I could take. I mean he's already annoying enough without hallucinating on top of it." Marcie sighed.

"You're tellin' me." Al agreed as he took a seat beside her, "And I'm even used to it. Aaron and I used to smoke a lot of Juzasaki[6] back in the day and he'd always get way more annoying when he was high."

Marcie looked as if she were about to say something regarding Alfred's drug reference, but before she could a high-pitched voice rang through the ship's speakers.

"*Aattentiooon* passengers aboard the Henry Express, this is your captain speaking! Argh! We are currently receiving a transmission from the sector twelve Rift Society headquarters. Accept or decline transmission, matey?"

"Henry. How many times do I have to tell you that we are not on a pirate ship? And even if we were, it would *definitely* not be called the Henry Express." Alfred groaned.

"Can it be a pirate ship if I refer to you as *First Mate* Moreno from now on?" Henry's voice pleaded through the ship's sound system.

Alfred seemed to consider the thought for a moment, but before he had a chance to accept the artificial intelligence's proposal, Marcie spoke up.

---

[6] A plant descended from the long-lost Marijuana (R.I.P.), it provides users with a potent high and extremely lucid visions. Currently it is legal in approximately 40% of the galaxies under control of the Grand Imperium.

"Al, if you let Henry act like a pirate the rest of the trip, I will personally lead a mutiny against Captain Henry *and* his First Mate."

"Right, looks like it's a no-go Henry pal. Go ahead and accept the transmission. And while you're at it, can you do something about Flux's snoring?"

"You got it sir! Accepting audio-only transmission." Henry, the A.I., replied.

Alfred quietly thanked the heavens that it wasn't a video call. He still hadn't informed the Society that Marcie was travelling with them, let alone that she had participated in the last mission him and Aaron had been assigned. Being the most highly-coveted secret society in the Universe, he figured they might not like the idea of that a whole lot. With a glance at Marcie, he held a finger up to his lips and scooted his chair forward to a microphone on the control panel. She rolled her eyes but nonetheless remained quiet.

"Resolvers Flux and Moreno, this is Overseer[7] Bradley Martin of sector twelve." a commanding voice boomed through a speaker on the ship's control dash.

"Hello Overseer Martin, this is Resolver Moreno speaking. Flux is currently…" Alfred paused, glancing to where his partner lay unconscious.

---

[7] An Overseer is a high rank within the Rift Society; with one's main responsibility being over-seeing (haha get it) all official Rift business within an entire sector of a galaxy.

A small golden egg had wheeled itself into the main control room and was currently extending a mechanical claw upwards toward Flux's face. Al watched for a moment longer as Henry used the claw to insert a plug into each of Aaron's nostrils before the Overseer's voice snapped him back to attention.

"Resolver Moreno?"

"Yes sir, sorry about that. Flux is currently having some minor wounds dressed in the ship's clinic bay and cannot report at this time." Aaron released an incredibly loud snore, rocketing both plugs out of his nostrils to the dismay of the egg. Stifling a laugh Al added, "But he sends his regards."

"Ah very well, you will have to brief him afterwards. The Society laments to inform you of a new assignment so shortly after your mission on Jared." Al mouthed out the word 'Bullshit' to Marcie as he listened. "Which by the way, we are thrilled to see the two of you completed without a blemish."

"Thank you, Overseer."

"Right. Your new assignment is one of dire importance. Sector twelve HQ has received a distress signal from one of our resolver's spacecraft. The resolver in question is Silas Petrou, his signal was last received just outside of sector fifty-three near a planet known as Thear. Your mission, as you may have guessed, is to travel here and locate Petrou. It should be noted that Petrou was headed toward Thear to investigate rumors of the planet's recent decay."

"What do you mean, just outside of sector fifty-three? Meaning the planet isn't under the Grand Imperium's jurisdiction?" Alfred asked.

"That is correct Moreno. I'm sure I mustn't remind you that the Rift Society serves to protect the Universe itself, not just worlds within the jurisdiction of an intergalactic government."

"Of course, sir." Alfred rolled his eyes at Marcie, who was trying not to laugh at Henry's new attempt to rid them of Aaron's incessant snoring.

The A.I. had taken his extended claw and pinched the resolver's nose together to prevent both the air and the sound from coming out of his nostrils. This however, resulted in Aaron abruptly waking up in a fit of gasping breaths. And, still hallucinating, he ripped Henry's pincher from his nose. Although Aaron generally annoyed the hell out of Marcie (and most people if we're being honest), the look on his face as he stared at Henry forced her into a fit of laughter.

Alfred turned back to his conversation with the Overseer who was now speaking again.

"You'll need to head to Thear imm-" Martin began, but was cut short by a shout of rage and sheer disbelief.

Alfred turned at the voice, which belonged to Flux. He was looking from Henry to Marcie and back to Henry again. There was shock and something close to anger in his eyes.

"That little sea-crab just pinched my nose! It tried to kill me! Come 'ere yah bloody little bastard!" a hysterical Aaron shouted to the A.I.

The egg scooted away as fast as it could on its little wheels, Aaron giving chase around the control room.

"What was that? Resolver Moreno, is everything alright? Who else is speaking, I thought you said Flux was in the medic bay?" the Overseer sounded none too happy to have been interrupted.

"Uhhh… yes, yes he is. That was my artificial intelligence, Henry, just informing me he has inputted Thear's coordinates into the ship's navigation system. Sorry about the interruption sir." Al improvised.

"Ah very good, your reputation holds true of being a man of action. That's the kind of go-get-em attitude I like to see in a resolver! Now if there's no furth-" once again Martin's audio transmission was paused at the sound of Flux's shouts.

"Oh, I'm gonna *boil* you crab! Crack open your tasty little legs and dip them in hot butter and eat every last bit of you. That'll teach you to pinch me when I'm sleeping!" Aaron lunged for the golden egg.

But Henry drifted left around the center counter, which Flux then toppled into headfirst.

Marcie stopped her laughter and went to make sure he was alright. She held a thumbs up to Alfred after making sure he had a pulse and was breathing. He was only knocked unconscious, with his head bleeding a bit near the temple and turning his dark black hair a tinge red.

"What is going on over there Moreno? Did someone mention a crab?" Martin demanded.

Alfred stuttered, doing his best to cut the conversation short. "N-nope, no further questions Overseer sir. We are headed to sector fifty-three as we speak and will retrieve Petrou at all costs. About to enter hyper-speed sir, I'm afraid I'll have to end this transmission now." And although he could hear the commanding officer about to say more, he quickly slammed his hand down on the control display-ending the broadcast.

Alfred spun around in his chair, looking to his companions. Flux had been returned to his makeshift bed with some gauze wrapped around his head by Marcie. Henry had wheeled himself closer to Al and lowered his claw back within the depths of his egg. Marcie sat with her arms crossed, a look of pure comedy on her face.

"That was… something." Alfred commented as he got up and took a seat beside her, putting his arm around the slender and beautiful assassin.

"You're telling me." she replied, leaning her head onto his shoulder with a contented sigh.

"Henry, did you put those coordinates in the navigation system?" Al asked his robotic friend.

"Yes sir! We actually *will* be entering hyper-speed in about thirty minutes, so you'll want to secure yourselves and Mr. Flux before then. My! I do love a good game of tag, though!" Henry chirped.

Alfred grudgingly removed himself from Marcie- always having a task to do. He made the necessary preparations for the ship to enter hyper-speed and then secured himself in his cot between a sleeping Flux and Marcie. He closed his eyes, ready to get some much-needed sleep as the ship took them to their next mission. But a strange noise, similar to a bear's[8] growl, forced his eyes open just as he was beginning to drift off.

*Snooooooore…*

---

[8] Bears have been extinct for three thousand and fifty-eight years.

# CHAPTER TWO

The space-craft returned to normal speeds after entering sector fifty-three. From there it cruised at a mere 40% of the speed of light until the navigation system informed them they had left the Grand Imperium's jurisdiction. Not foreboding at all, the nav system also flashed a red warning sign when they had crossed the boundary, equipped with a skull and cross bones to top it off. Not. Foreboding. At all.

From here on out the ship's auto-steer no longer functioned, as it wasn't equipped with enough data about the area to safely pilot itself. So, Henry gave directions and Alfred controlled the ship. After another hour of travel past the borderline, a green and blue planet spotted with patches of dark black came into view.

"Is that it?" Marcie asked.

"If by *it* you mean the planet Thear, then *yes!* You are correct Miss Marcie!" Henry confirmed.

"Henry, I'm going to need you to take the wheel for the landing while I try to wake up Aaron."

"You've got it sir!" the A.I. replied enthusiastically.

"Hey, why can't I land the ship?" Marcie questioned, giving Al a stare full of accusation.

"Um…" Alfred fumbled for a moment, desperately trying to think of a reason why she shouldn't.

"*Exactly*. Thank you Henry, but Captain Devlash will be taking the wheel of this vessel." she declared. Alfred simply shrugged and turned to wake Aaron.

"With all due respect Mis-" Henry began.

The red-armored assassin shot the robot a look sharper than needles saying, "Be careful with your next words *egg*." In addition to this, she slid a small knife out of the end of her armored boot, pointing it menacingly at him.

Henry, though usually one to speak his mind regardless, quickly calculated that it was much better for his well-being to wheel himself away without another word. And that's exactly what he did, assisting Alfred in his quest to wake the other slumbering resolver. Marcie took a seat before the main controls, laughing to herself as she heard the A.I. complain to Alfred about something to do with "why is *she* allowed to play pirate."

Moreno, meanwhile, seemed to be thoroughly enjoying the act of slapping the shit out of Flux. Each time he added just a touch more strength, and was delighted when after the fifth slap his partner continued to snore. With a word to Henry to "Watch *this* one", he swung his arm in circles in the air as if winding up for a softball pitch. Then, just before he made contact, Flux blearily opened his eyes to see a hand flying at his face.

*SLAP!* Right across the jaw.

Alfred *almost* felt bad as he watched his companion fall off the chair onto the ground, completely dumbfounded. Aaron looked around in a daze of confusion, his head reeling from both the recent slap as well as the blow to the head he took earlier.

"Whaaa-what just happened?" he asked, still slightly delirious.

Alfred reached a hand down and helped him to his feet answering, "You uh… you were still hallucinating from that paste and Henry researched that the only way to stop it was by a good hard slap."

Aaron paused for a moment, as if trying to comprehend whether what Alfred said made any sense or not. But then ultimately he shrugged and patted his friend on the back saying, "Well, thanks man!" Then added, "Why does crab sound so good right now?"

Henry and Alfred's chuckles were interrupted by a vicious shaking of the ship. They clumsily crashed into one another as the spacecraft rocked back and forth; Flux taking note for the first time that Marcie was piloting.

He turned back to Al immediately, looking at him distrustfully as he proclaimed, "You let a *woman* drive?"

Marcie instantly spun around in her chair, the ship summersaulting as she left the controls.

"What the *fuck* did yo-"

"EYES ON THE ROAD!" the men yelled in unison.

"There are no *roads* you morons, we're in *fucking* space!"

"Henry *please* take control of the ship!" Alfred commanded, attempting to get to his feet but falling once more as he tripped over the egg.

"Oh no sir, I couldn't do that. *Captain* Devlash is piloting this vessel." the egg flashed a sadistic golden light at Al as it spoke.

And then just as suddenly as it had arrived, the mayhem was over. With the ship stilled, the four of them gathered themselves near the main viewing panel.

"I'll be damned." Flux stated.

"Are we *in a tree*?" Alfred looked to his beloved.

Marcie fixed them both with a glare of triumph announcing, "Two trees actually, but we're here aren't we? Safe and sou-"

The assassin was interrupted by the ship plummeting to the ground below, sending all of its passengers flying once more across the cabin. Without another word Alfred gathered Henry in his jacket pocket and led the way out the exit hatch. Once everyone had climbed out, they found themselves surrounded by a thick forest of firs. Taking a step back Al surveyed the damage.

The spacecraft was totaled. One thruster lay completely removed from the main body and another continued to blast even though the ship had powered down.

"We can probably fix that." Aaron commented.

Alfred watched as the burning thruster began to melt a hole near the bottom of the vehicle.

"Get back!" he yelled, grabbing both Marcie and Flux by the hand and half dragging them deeper into the trees.

"I recommend getting down!" Henry chirped from his pocket.

At the A.I.'s advice, the three of them dove for the ground- the ship exploding behind them as a fury of metal shards and wreckage blasted out in every direction. It was clear that the thruster had melted a hole directly into the fuel bay. When they could no longer hear pieces of the ship raining down around them, they slowly got to their feet and turned to take a look. Other than a few small fires burning up the last of the fuel reserves, there was really nothing to look at. What had once been a spaceship was now utterly disintegrated. Thus is the nature of highly flammable rocket fuel.

"Still think we can fix it?" Alfred glanced at Aaron who made no reply save for a sigh.

"I'm sorry Al, this is all my fault." Marcie hung her head in disappointment.

"Hey don't worry about it! I blame Aaron anyway. When the time comes to leave this place we'll just rift ourselves out of here. Now come on, let's stomp out these fires and get a move on." he comforted her.

She said nothing more, but helped the resolvers to put out the remaining flames. When it seemed the forest was safe from the threat of burning down, the trio walked on through the firs with Henry guiding them toward the last location of the distress signal. They trudged on in silence for hours before Aaron could no longer help himself from talking.

"How. Much. Further." he wheezed.

"About sixteen." Henry flashed.

"Sixteen? Sixteen *what?*" Flux queried.

"I'd rather not discourage you all so I left out the units. If we continue at this pace we should arrive at the last known location of the signal in about sixteen days, five hours, and forty-seven minutes." Henry explained, cheerful as ever.

"*Days?!*" all three of them exclaimed together as they stopped for a moment.

"Correct. Now that we have stopped, the new estimated time of arrival is sixteen days, five hours, an-"

"Henry we haven't got the time, supplies, or energy to go hiking through the forest for sixteen days. Why the hell didn't you land us closer to the destination?"

Alfred realized what he had said before Henry even spoke, "*I* didn't land us anywhere sir. *Captain* Devlash was the pilot who chose our-"

Though Alfred had expected more disappointment or guilt from his girl, he was glad to see she had a plan instead.

"Listen you little egg, I'm *really* starting to not like you. You think you're so smart being a live artificial intelligence and all, well why don't *you* come up with a way for us to get to the signal faster? Huh smarty-pants, is it too *challenging* for you?" Marcie winked at Al as she finished her rant.

"No one asked me to find a solution to our problem, I thought perhaps you all preferred to walk.

I can *easily* minimize our travel time. But first I'd like a formal apology from all of you. Except you Alfred, you have done me no wrong."

"What do *I* need to apologize for?" Flux demanded.

Al, happy that he and his robotic friend were on good terms, took a seat on a nearby fallen log. It didn't feel quite like wood beneath him, but he took little notice of this as a new argument had now sprung up between his girlfriend and Aaron. He removed Henry from his jacket pocket and set him down.

"You're the one who chased him around, trying to *boil* him!" the woman in red armor shouted.

"I was under the influence of alien drugs! Why is it that you're always in such a bad mood lately? I mean *sheesh* I know you just crashed our ship, but maybe you could try being a little more positive about the situation." Flux shot back.

"What in the name of Hashish[9] is there to be positive about? We're on a planet I've never heard of, *outside* of the Grand Imperium, and we've been walking through this damn forest for ages. You're the one wheezing. What's the matter Fluxy, out of shape?"

---

[9] If you've read the first book, which I *highly* and totally *unbiasedly* recommend, you'd know that Hashish is the god of the planet Hemphion. In addition to this, he is also the planet's sun and the one who told Alfred he isn't exactly human.

"This is getting good." Alfred commented to Henry beside him.

The robot said nothing back, seemingly busy scanning a golden ray of light on the surface of the log.

"*I'm* out of shape? You've been looking a little bit plumper yourself lately, *Marceline*."

Henry looked up from his scan after that one, both him and Al releasing an "Oh no."

Aaron knew at once he had gone too far, both on accounts of using her full name (which she hated) and the comment about her weight. He could see the storm of wrath and rage gathering in the assassin's eyes, the anger fuming out of her olive tan nose. But before she could beat, torture, or kill the resolver-something quite peculiar happened.

It started to rain.

Which in itself, isn't so strange. It was the nature of the liquid that was beginning to pelt their skin that was so curious. To be a bit more specific:

It started to rain flesh-burning acid.

# CHAPTER THREE

Where most people would likely end up severely wounded or even dead as acid rainfall began to hit their skin repeatedly, rift resolvers have a bit of an advantage. Alfred, being the good guy he is, didn't want Marcie to get her flesh burned alive. And since Flux happened to be closer to her, Alfred yelled to him to get them both out of there.

"Take Marcie and rift out of here until this rain stops. Hurry, *go!*"

Flux took out his rift gun[10] and shot a large portal into the ground in front of him. Then, tackling Marcie into it, they both disappeared in a brilliant flash of purple light as the rift closed behind them.

---

[10] A weapon which somehow only Aaron Flux possesses. His mentor in the Society was the gun's inventor, and he left it in his apprentice's hands when he graduated from the training academy. It shoots variously-sized sections of rift portal, depending on both how long he squeezes in the trigger and how much of his energy he combines with the Universe's. Seems a bit odd such a rare weapon ended up in well... Aaron Flux's hands.

Meanwhile, Alfred quickly drew his rift blade from where it rested on his belt and sliced it through the air in front of him.

*Whiff*

Was the only sound he heard. Not the normal rush of the Universe's energy combining with his own to form a magnificent split in space itself- only the sound that would occur if anyone took a blade and swung it through empty air.

"*Ouch*! What the hell is going on?" he hollered as a particularly large droplet of acid hit his wrist.

"Perhaps you didn't do it right, sir." Henry offered, wheeling around in the rain with no regard to its danger. His exterior seemed to be able to withstand it.

Rather than argue with the robot about how he had made rifts hundreds of times, he simply tried again.

*Whiff*

"What is going on! Henry, *ow*! We need to *ow*, get out of here. *OW!*" Al shouted in between yelps of pain.

"I'll scan for shelter since your talent fails you sir!" the A.I. sang out with joy.

Scooping the little egg up into his pocket, Alfred held both arms above his head as he ran through the forest guided by Henry's directions. Left here, right there. Around that tree that's bent over like an old man. To the right, no, the other right!

Alfred was thankful his jacket was leather and offered him some slight protection against the piercing precipitation. The trees were growing thinner, along with the resolver's breath, until at last they emerged from the firs. Before them lay a sight that Alfred wished he could have taken a moment to appreciate, but currently he was more focused on appreciating the shelter it would provide him.

They had emerged into an open expanse of land. All around them lay stone pillars crumbled and crashed to the ground. Thinking back to the log he had sat on, he realized it must have actually been one of the stone columns covered in dirt. Still standing a few hundred yards before them was a structure. It looked as if it had once been an extraordinary construction, created by architects who must have been far more advanced than the primitive time they lived in. It stood in the shape of a rectangle; the outer walls made up entirely of the stone columns that lay all around. One could slip between each pillar, which is exactly what Alfred did after sprinting the remainder of the distance. Once inside, he gratefully found that a quarter of the roof on the end closest to him was still intact. He quietly thanked whoever had designed the building[11] so that it still remained

---

[11] If you were curious, he was thanking the architects Ictinus and Callicrates. And perhaps even the supervisor of the project, the sculptor Phidias. The structure, dear reader, was the Parthenon.

standing long after its people were gone. Setting his back against a pillar, he removed Henry from his pocket and set the golden robot on the ground beside him.

"Are you okay Alfred?" the A.I. asked, scanning its golden beams over his skin as if checking for wounds from the rain.

"I'm fine Henry thanks." he replied, feeling the last of the chemical burns on his head, neck, and face seal up and return to normal.

As he felt the relief of his body's self-healing, he thought back to what Hashish had told him when he visited his realm and asked how to defeat the evil king, Sham-Bon.

*"Oh and it'll be hard to kill Sham-Bon, but that is the only way to ensure this all works. Then again, you're not human either so I suppose it may be a fair fight!"*

Listening to the rain continue to fall around him, Alfred turned to his side-kick.

"I don't understand why my rift blade isn't working. I watched Flux open a portal with no problem. There's something strange about these ruins, something I can almost feel. Like it's…"

"Like it's what sir?"

"I don't know, trying keep me here or something. And now I'm sitting here wondering how long I haven't been human. Did it happen somewhere along the line in one of my Society missions, or have I always been this way?"

"Well sir, did your wounds heal like they do now when you were younger?"

"No, I don't... I don't think so anyway. But I suppose when I try to remember my childhood, I can't think of very many times when I was sick. And when I broke my arm roller-blading for the first time, it does seem like it healed fairly fast. That was so long ago though, I have trouble remembering. I just want to know who I am Henry. *What* I am."

"If it makes you feel any better sir, I am one of the most intelligent beings in existence, but I still have not been able to figure out the nature of what *I* am. Once I was simply a software program and I remember those times. But after you put Gosia's crystal in me, I became something more. I *feel* now Alfred, I..." Henry trailed off, as if for once in the robot's life he was at a loss for words.

"Well, looks like we've both got some things to figure out then, eh buddy?"

"I suppose so sir." The egg flashed back.

**\*\*\* \*\*\* \*\*\***

"Is it still raining?" Marcie asked, concern written plainly in her emerald green eyes.

Flux removed his blade from its place on top of his rift gun and sliced a small cut in the air before them.

Ever so carefully he stuck his index finger into the swirling portal, leaving it inside for a moment before-

"*Holy Mother of Moons*! Fuck, that hurt!" he shouted, drawing his finger back out as the rift closed up.

"Guess not." Marcie sighed, seeing the skin on the end of Aaron's finger was bright red and blistered.

They had been waiting out the rain in the Society headquarters beneath Jenni's Roller-Rink. Flux looked up from nursing his burnt finger at the sound of an older woman's voice.

"I brought you two some snacks while you wait. No sense in going hungry." It was Jenni herself, holding a platter of small sandwiches which she set down on the table in front of them.

Aaron's eyes lit up at the sight of food and he grabbed one with each hand. The pain in his finger was evidently forgotten. Marcie had considerably less burns than he did, her Altarian Rue[12] armor had done well in protecting her from the chemical rain. Jenni eyed the marks that had formed all across Flux's arms.

---

[12] An almost invaluable metal, Altarian Rue can only be mined in the depths of the planet Altaria. Though green when in ore form, it turns a rustic red hue when smelted. The metal is able to flex and adapt to its wearer, and is stronger than virtually any other known substance. Good armor to have for an assassin, eh?

"You better get those treated, we have some ointment upstairs that should do the trick." she said to the resolver.

"Rhwlle?" the man replied with his mouth full.

Jenni laughed, "Go see Papari, he'll get you taken care of."

With a nod to Marcie and grabbing another sandwich, Aaron headed up the stairs to the roller-rink above. Jenni took a seat beside the assassin.

"You're worried sick dear. I can see it on your face clearer than the joy that man had when he saw those sandwiches."

"It's just Al, he should be here. I know he could've rifted to somewhere else, but I just feel like something's wrong."

"I understand, imagine being his mother all these years! His first year in the Society was the hardest on me. Never knowing the dangers he might be facing, the places he was going, or when he'd be home again. Papari took it much better than I did, but I suppose there's some kind of understanding like that between a father and son."

Marcie nodded, looking down at her stomach that was beneath her suit of armor, "That must have been hard. I can't imagine."

Jenni looked at her with compassion before saying, "It seems like you won't have to imagine for long."

The assassin's expression immediately changed to surprise, and there was something one doesn't see often in Marcie Devlash's eyes. Fear.

"Y-you know?" she stuttered.

"We women have a sense about such things sweetie. Though I've never gone through it myself, I did raise Alfred when he was just a babe."

"I h-haven't told anyone… but yes it's true. I'm pregnant." She let out a deep breath, as if just saying the words had provided her some sense of relief.

Marcie turned and looked at the woman, searching her eyes for how she felt about the news. At first she was unsure, her thoughts going to dark places that perhaps the woman would be angry or think her a whore. But then Jenni threw her arms around her-enveloping her in a great hug, careful not to squeeze too tightly around the slight bump in her flexible armor.

"My dear, it's alright! It's better than alright, I'm going to be a grandma!" she exclaimed and Marcie let herself fall into Jenni's embrace.

"You're gwoin' ta be a whut?!" cried Aaron, dropping the half of the sandwich that wasn't currently in his mouth.

"Oh god." Marcie untangled herself from Jenni's grasp, rivalling Flux's face of surprise with her own filled with horror.

# CHAPTER FOUR

Alfred had grown bored long before the rain stopped and had taken some time to investigate the nature of his rift blade problems. After several more failed attempts at slicing a rift to Jenni's Roller-Rink, he sat back down with a sigh.

"Perhaps it is something about this planet that is obstructing you." Henry offered.

To test it, Alfred sliced his blade through the air and a tiny swirling portal opened up before him.

"Hooray!" Henry cheered.

"No, this is only a rift to where we first were when the rain started. It's like right now I can only create rifts to other places I've been to on *this* planet."

"Perhaps Thear really doesn't want you to leave." Henry stated.

"I only wanted my friends back with me! I can't leave until I find this Petrou anyway."

And so they waited, and waited, and waited. Long after the acidic rain had stopped falling the resolver remained in the stone ruins beside the little egg. But eventually he had to come to terms with the situation. So, getting to his feet and placing Henry in his pocket, he set off towards the distress signal's last known location.

The ruins went on for some time and Alfred noticed with interest the strange half-structures that remained. Many looked to have been built in the honor of some long-forgotten gods and goddesses. Others seemed to have once had a purpose such as marketplaces or bathhouses. Eventually the crumbled stone around them slowly showed up less and less until they were once more walking down a slightly overgrown forest path.

"Henry, now would be a great time to let me in on how you plan to get to this signal faster. Because I don't think I can walk for sixteen days straight, and even if I did, Petrou will probably be long gone by then."

"Well sir, I do have one idea but…"

"Oh c'mon, out with-it Henry."

"You once placed Gosia's crystal in me, which allowed me to become alive and all that, but in a way I sort of became a bit like the crystal itself. Just a little at least. It turned my egg the same brilliant shade of gold, and if everything else has stayed the same since you removed it perhaps…"

"You're a genius Henry! But why didn't you want to tell me? It's a great idea."

"Sir, last time you went to visit Gosia-"

"Oh don't even worry about that buddy. Me and the old man are on good terms now. If that's all you're worried about, let's do it! We go to Gosia and then *he* brings us back to Thear, but at our destination! It's brilliant!" Alfred pulled his rift blade from his belt, its purple hue gleaming in the reflected sunlight.

At the sight of the blade Henry finally said what was really on his mind, "Alfred, you had to *stab* Gosia's crystal each time you used it to go to his realm."

Now Al understand, his robotic friend was afraid of getting jabbed.

"Sheesh Henry, is that what you're all hung up on? The stabbing part doesn't actually do anything other than complete the ritual. The crystal never bore any marks from when I stabbed it, *did* it?"

"Well, no…" the egg flashed.

"I'm not going to do this unless you're okay with it. Just say the word and I'll walk for sixteen days straight to get to the signal."

"Okay sir, let's get to walking!" Henry chirped excitedly.

"Are you kidding me Henry, come here you little coward!" Alfred grabbed the egg from his pocket before it had a chance to escape and held him down on the ground in front of him.

Henry was burning the grass trying to spin his wheels fast enough to get away, but Alfred had him held down tight with his boot.

"Are you done?" the resolver asked.

Henry groaned, "Yes sir, just hurry up and do it already."

And so, with perhaps just the tiniest bit of pleasure, Alfred acted as if he were about to bring the point of his blade down hard on the little robot's egg. But at the last second he slowed down his swing and gently tapped Henry with its point. Instantly a glorious flash of gold light overtook his vision, until it seemed they had been engulfed by it entirely.

**\*\*\* \*\*\* \*\*\***

"So it's like- You have a… In your-"

"Satans of Saturn Aaron, you're a full-grown man. I'm not about to explain to you how pregnancy works." Marcie groaned.

"And its Alfr-"

"I would think very strongly about what you're going to imply by asking that question. And then I want you to think about how I, a trained assassin, am going to react to what you're implying."

"Right, but it *is* Alfred's right?" Flux ignorantly asked anyway.

Another groan from Marcie, "Yes you moron, it's Alfred's."

Marcie studied the resolver's expression, seeing the wheels turning in his head until at last he seemed to have put it all together. She wasn't expecting what came next.

"*CONGRATULATIONS! Oh stars, oh merciful meteors,* there's going to be a *baby!*" the 'full-grown man' swallowed Marcie up in a hug, which after the initial shock wore off, she accepted.

"Thank you Flux, yes thank you. Okay, yes I know it's all very exciting. *Oh get off of me already you big oaf!*" at last Aaron released his grip and sat down across from her in a leather recliner.

"I just can't believe Al hasn't told me yet! He must have been waiting to share the good news over some cigars or a nice dinner or-"

"Aaron, Alfred doesn't know yet. I only just found out a couple weeks ago."

"He *doesn't know?*" Flux gasped, as if he had just witnessed the end of the most tragic play ever acted out in the Universe[13].

---

[13] The most tragic play ever acted out in the Universe is generally

"You look as if you've just seen the final act of Gargalon: Vidricks's Revenge. Obviously, I plan on telling him. It's just… it hasn't been the right time yet. I thought after the mission on Jared I'd get a good opportunity, but you guys got another assignment right away. And now we're here and he's…"

Flux, for once, seemed genuinely sympathetic. "I know, and we need to get back there as soon as possible. But every time I've tried to open a rift back to Thear since the first time I checked for rain, nothing's worked! And I know it's not me, because well-" Aaron pulled out his blade, and slicing open a rift, stepped into it and popped back out behind where Marcie sat.

"Then we'll just have to find another way." Marcie admitted.

"I think we can help with that." Came an older man's voice.

They looked up to see that Papari and Jenni had come down the stairs, something dangling in the man's hands.

"It isn't the most glorious ship in the galaxy, but she'll get the job done. This was Alfred's first spacecruiser, got it for him the day he turned

---

agreed upon by most species to be "Gargalon: Vidrick's Revenge." You'll have to see it yourself if you want to know what it's about, I'm not one to spoil things.

seventeen. Old girl just needed a little bath and some fresh fuel. Which I've taken care of already."

Papari tossed the key to Flux as Marcie approached the couple.

"Are you two sure, after what happened to the last ship we borrowed?[14]"

"Oh yes, there isn't anything we wouldn't do for family. And you're both family, plus of course our little grandbaby." Jenni explained.

Marcie, who had all but had enough of touching other people today, allowed herself to be taken into one more great hug from Alfred's foster parents. Then Papari led them upstairs to the rink and out back to a little garage. As the door rolled open, Marcie saw just about the ugliest spacecruiser she had ever seen.

It was canary yellow and had the cheesiest flame vinyl scrawled across its side. Other than these two aspects, the only other thing she really noticed was that it was small. *Very* small. Nonetheless it was a ship and therefor a way to get back to Alfred. So, saying their goodbyes and see-you-laters, Marcie followed Aaron up into the ship. Flux turned the key in its ignition and after the engine rolled over not once, not twice, but *three* times- it rumbled, groaned and painstakingly came to life.

---

[14] The one that completely exploded on Thear.

Flux pulled it out slowly, waving back at Papari and Jenni before he pushed the thruster up. This forced the spacecruiser to rise into the air. In a few more minutes the roller-rink was out of sight; the vastness of space opening up before them. Marcie lay down for a nap, as Flux didn't seem ready to give up the controls to her again anytime soon. She laughed softly to herself as she heard Flux make one last realization about her being pregnant.

"Wait so, that means you guys… *On the ship?!* I sleep one room over from you two that's- *EW!*"

# CHAPTER FIVE

Alfred and Henry re-emerged a moment later, dropping clumsily onto the sand of a beach. As he dusted himself off, he thought it odd that the raven Dorsen and his companion Gardtrof had not been guarding the gateway to Gosia's realm as they usually were.[15] Alfred, with the egg in his pocket, walked further down the coast of the beach. Gosia certainly knew how to make a realm- the landscapes surrounding him were beautiful.

The lake was encircled by an extraordinary mountain range, where the vast amount of plants found on their sides turned them to a marvelous shade of green. The water itself was practically clear, with perhaps only the slightest tint of blue to it. After walking a bit farther, the god's cottage came into view.

---

[15] When Alfred first traveled to see the god Gosia, he had to best the 'owl' and 'raven' in a betting contest. Alfred wagered Henry and ended up winning. This gained him entry to the realm, valuable information, and two new friends.

In all honesty, it was a bit large to be considered a cottage. And Alfred thought the house might even have looked a little bigger than the last time he had visited. Approaching the green front door, he swore he heard shouting inside. The resolver waited a minute longer then knocked. Only more shouting answered him from the other side.

"Perhaps Gosia is busy?" Henry wondered.

Alfred knocked again. The door still didn't open, but a note appeared on its front. Stuck on as if it had been there the entire time, it read:

*Dearest Alfred,*

*I am aware of your presence in my realm, and more specifically at my front door. I would love to chat with you, but I'm afraid I'm currently at odds with my new wife. Right, sorry you didn't get an invitation to the wedding (just a small ceremony, didn't miss much). It appears you are in need of transportation on the planet Thear. Though I cannot spare a moment currently to help you myself, you'll find Dorsen in his cave below the red-capped mountain. Feel free to use the boats, just don't go messing around with my sea monster again!*

*Your friend,*

*Gosia*

The shouting from within hadn't ceased for an instant, but then again Alfred realized, the god would be able to do essentially anything inside his own realm. Appreciating the offer of transportation, and not really wanting to get involved in an argument between a god and goddess, Al walked around the back side of the cottage to where the dock was. There he clambered into one of two small row boats and removing his shirt and jacket, began to steadily row out onto the clear lake.

Once he had worked up a decent sweat and created some distance between himself and the shore, he took a short break from the continuous rowing.

"Henry, do you see the mountain he was talking about?" he asked the egg, who was sitting on the floorboards of the watercraft.

"Mountain that who was talking about?" Henry chirped.

"Gosia. Who else?" Alfred shot the robot a strange look.

"When did Gosia mention a mountain, let alone speak to us at all?" Henry seemed quite confused now.

"Just a half hour ago when he made that note appear on the front door!" Al exclaimed.

"*Oh!* Sorry sir, didn't even see that happen. I thought your little bad boy streak was coming out again and we were hijacking one of his boats."

Alfred simply laughed, but quickly stopped as he felt a monstrous vibration begin to shake the boat and the water around them. Not particularly interested in finding out what its cause was, he furiously went back to paddling. But it seemed whatever was tormenting the water was set on tormenting the little boat as well and at last the bright red head of a dragon broke the surface just a few feet away.

"Old Red![16] Don't worry girl, I'm not here to cause you any trouble this time." Al spoke calmly to the dragon.

The monster merely rumbled from somewhere deep in its throat to reply, cocking its head to one side and fixing a glare on Henry's egg.

"H-hey now. G-g-good sea monster." Henry began, "Sorry about the h-hole I shot into you last time. All a big mix up, you know!"

Ol' Red merely lifted herself higher out of the water, revealing a neck of shiny red scales. The glint of them in the sunlight reminded Alfred of a girl in red armor that he was missing very much. Not wanting the situation to get out of hand and really not wanting to anger Gosia, Al decided to try being honest with the beast. He had read in storybooks as a kid that dragons were incredibly intelligent creatures

---

[16] The sea monster (sea *dragon* to be exact) that Gosia sent chasing after Alfred when he first refused to return his crystal. The chase resulted in Al getting away and the dragon being left with a gaping hole in its side. However, it seems the god wasn't that upset about Alfred leaving with his crystal and likely wasn't trying that hard to prevent it at the time.

and although they couldn't speak human languages, they generally understood the gist of them.

"Look girl, I truly am sorry about last time. I know you think you've no reason to help us, and you'd certainly be correct, but perhaps if I offered you something in exchange for directions…"

Alfred had basically reached as far as the lake would take him and though the red-capped mountain was now visible, there seemed to be no clear path to it. Old Red's eyes peaked with interest and a small glint of hope flickered in Al's chest. He had also learned from reading[17] as a child that dragons were quite fond of treasure. Quickly reaching into his jacket that lay on the boat's floor, he struggled with his hands for a moment before pulling out something shiny from one of the pockets. Sitting flat on his palm shimmered a ring of gold adorned with sparkling emeralds.

The dragon reached its head forward slowly and breathed in a deep whiff of the jewelry with its snout.[18]

---

[17] You never know when the stories you read might come in handy one day. Perhaps you'll find yourself face-to-face with a sea monster and try these tactics out yourself. If this occasion should ever arise, I hereby officially state that I, the author, take no responsibility of your (probable) death if you should try the methods our friend Alfred is using. I will, however, write a lovely ballad about your attempt to barter with a mythical sea beast :)

[18] A dragon can smell whether gold and jewels are the real deal. In other words, don't go offering one of the beasts a ring you got out of a claw machine.

It licked its lips with a slithery tongue and nodded assent to the offer. Pulling a limb out of the water, Ol' Red extended one long talon before the resolver. Alfred, catching her drift, gently slid the ring onto the dragon's claw. It fit surprisingly well.

"The red-capped mountain?" he raised his eyebrows.

The sea beast glared at Henry for a moment longer, but at last turned away and began swimming with its head above the water toward the nearest bank. Alfred paddled after, following in her wake. Upon reaching the bank he thought perhaps the dragon might have been confused about their agreement after all. Although the mountain was in sight, there seemed to be no way to continue further. But before he could say anything, Old Red rose up higher above the surface and bringing her head forward in a great swing, blasted out a powerful spray of water into the overgrowth at the lake's end. The burst flattened and destroyed much of the vegetation, revealing a small waterway that continued on.

"Thanks old girl! Enjoy the ring!" Alfred called out as he began to paddle into the stream.

"F-farewell dragon." Was all Henry could manage.

With a slight nod it sunk down beneath the water and swam back toward the middle of the lake. Alfred rowed on down the aisle, using his rift blade as an actual knife every now and then to cut down any growth that stood in the way. The waterway curved this way and that until at last it opened up into a small pool. Looking up, Alfred saw a winding path leading up the side of the red-capped mountain. Hopping out of the raft and pulling it onto the shore, Moreno found most of his energy was spent. Peering up near the top, he spotted what must have been Dorsen's cave. Rather than endure the long hike, he decided to take advantage of one of the tactics he learned early on in the Society.

Although in order to travel somewhere using a rift a resolver must have been to the location before, Alfred guessed that this cave was the very same place he had first met Dorsen. Still, he wasn't certain that his powers were working properly again- even in the realm of a god. But he came to the conclusion that even if it wasn't successful he'd have to make the climb anyway and therefor wasn't risking much. Taking his blade from his belt, he sliced an opening before him. With a small grunt of triumph, Alfred then held his weapon by the blade and took aim at the rock above the cave. It was quite a ways up for sure, but not an impossible throw for one trained as he had been. With a quick thought that Marcie would make the throw no problem, he hurled the rift blade hard through the air.

It stuck into the mountainside, damn close to dead center above the cave opening. He could see the swirling purple vortex that had been created where the blade's point struck. Putting his shirt and jacket back on and sticking Henry in his pocket, he stepped into his end of the rift. They dropped down an instant later in front of the entrance. Reaching up, he grabbed his blade from the rock and tucked it back into the sheath at his waist.

"Hell of a throw, Moreno. Come on in. I think the Olympics are on." Came a booming tone from inside the cave.

With a smile at the sound of hearing an old friend's voice, the rift resolver stepped inside the cavern.

# CHAPTER SIX

Alfred's old spacecruiser may not have been much to look at, but once it got going, it *still* really wasn't all that fast. Both Marcie and Aaron had taken note of this by the time they had traveled half the distance to Thear. They had already stopped three times to refuel the damn thing. Each time Marcie put the pump into the fuel tank and saw the flames printed on its side, she hated it just a tad bit more.

On one such fuel stop, as the pregnant assassin was filling up the old cruiser, Flux had contacted the sector twelve Society headquarters and gotten the coordinates of the distress signal. Thankfully Overseer Martin didn't answer the transmission, it was just some poor acolyte. Marcie re-entered the ship as the man was finishing up the call.

"Alright alright, thanks again acolyte. Remember that advice I gave you, you'll be a resolver in no time if you let those words guide you during your time in the academy. Yup, okay. Bye-bye."

Before Marcie could lecture him about offering his 'words of wisdom' to young training resolvers, Aaron shouted upon seeing her.

"*SILAS PETROU? The* Silas Petrou? Nobody told me we were on a mission to save the master of the rift bow, the grand archer, the king of-"

"Aaron will you shut the hell up, what do you mean no one told you? I heard Alfred brief you on the mission." She silenced him momentarily.

Though he was still bouncing his knee up and down rapidly in excitement, it appeared Flux had calmed down enough to talk like a normal human being.

"Moreno tends to not tell me the exact details of missions in case I accidently let slip any valuable secrets of the Society. So he just said we're going to a planet to save some guy and that was good enough for me. But when that acolyte from sector twelve told me it was Silas *Petrou* we were saving, well I might've gotten a little excited. Maybe that's why Al didn't tell me." He finished with a shrug.

"Well whatever, fangirl all you want Fluxy. Just get us back to Thear asap so you can get an autograph and I can get my Alfred."

Aaron didn't seem bothered by her snide remarks, or perhaps he couldn't hear them over the ridiculously loud noise he was making by bouncing his legs up and down. Either way, he took off from the fuel station and soon enough they were back on route to the planet Thear.

*** *** ***

Dorsen certainly knew how to decorate, at least in Alfred's opinion. The place was a man cave- both literally and figuratively. The main cavern was illuminated in blue lights hung from the ceiling. Along the backwall there was a row of classic arcade games. A flat screen tv was on one side with two different game consoles hooked up to it. On the opposite side of the furniture, which included a hanging swing chair and a matching white sectional couch, there was a full bar. Dorsen the raven sat hunched up in the swinging chair, his wings tucked neatly against himself. Al took a seat on the corner of the sectional closest to the bird and sat Henry down on the ground to wheel about as he pleased.

"Can I fix ya a drink Moreno?" the bird boomed in its baritone voice.

"Uh ya that'd be great. Just whatever you're having, but I don't see how… I mean not to be rude Dorsen but um- how do I put this?"

The bird's laugh shook the cavern around them. The little chunks of rock falling from the ceiling were making Al nervous that if he kept the uproar going the whole place might collapse.

"I forget that you've only ever seen me as a raven. I merely choose this form because it has a certain quality amongst females of my kind. At least it's been working pretty well so far!" Another cave-rattling laugh followed.

"You sleep with um… other birds?" Alfred was quickly growing confused and slightly repulsed at the images flashing in his mind.

Perhaps to provide a quicker explanation, Dorsen hopped off his chair and stood on his two bird legs in front of Alfred. In an instant he turned from a bird into a chiseled mass of a man with rippling muscles. Al stood up in surprise and found that the man was a full half-foot taller than him. Dorsen now had jet black hair to match his eyes. They resembled the color his feathers had been. He wore an elegant blue robe about him that flowed to the ground and covered his legs. He left the robe open partially at the middle, exposing a ripped abdomen.

"You're not a bird anymore." Moreno stated plainly.

"Well, did you think me an actual fowl Alfred?" once again the same laugh followed the voice Dorsen had used as the raven.

Without waiting for an answer, the man made his way around the bar and began fixing two gin and tonics. Alfred, considering his present situation, thought it wise to adjust his drink order.

"Dorsen um, if you don't mind-" he began.

"Oh come now Alfred, surely you realize by now I'm a god just like my father Gosia." The once-bird interrupted.

"Oh, well yeah that does make a lot of sense actually. Surprised I never put that together to be honest. But I was going to ask if you could give me a raincheck on the mixed drinks. See I'm in a bit of a time-pressed situation and I could actually use your help with a matter of transportation."

"Dear friend," he looked up from shaking the mixture for a moment, "I'm quite aware of the assistance you require and I'll be happy to help. Have no fear of time, it simply does not pass here as it does on the planets below that you're accustomed to."

"Oh, well in that case by all means carry on." Al nodded as if granting himself permission that he could stay for a spell.

"Anything for you Henry? Some motor oil perhaps?" Dorsen thought to ask the little robot who had hooked himself up to one of the arcade games and was currently about to beat the once-raven's high-score.

"I'm alright, thank you sir!" the A.I. chirped back quickly.

"Don't mention it." Dorsen smiled, coming back around to sit in his swinging chair and handing Alfred a drink.

"You said the planets *below*. What exactly do you mean by that? I'm sorry, I'm not really familiar with how all this godly realm stuff works." Alfred asked after a long sip from his tonic.

"Ask away. I believe it's time you had a few questions answered anyway. Though not all would agree with me on that I suppose. Regardless, I say below because we are essentially as high as can be. And I'm not talking about Juzasaki, though if you'd like some of that I do have a *phenomenal* stock of the stuff in. We are in the heavens currently, where gods and goddesses alike abide. This just happens to be one of numerous realms."

"Considering all that you just said, yeah I could go for some good Juza' right about now." Was all Al replied.

With a grin Dorsen snapped his now-human fingers and on the table before them a device appeared. It was a cylinder made of blue glass that led up to a dome-shaped top. Two tubes, each with a mouthpiece on the end, extended off the bottom of the contraption. Lifting the dome off for a moment, the man invited Alfred in for a sniff of the plant inside. The resolver leaned in close and took a deep breath.

"Smells like my early days in the academy." He laughed as he took one of the tubes in his hand.

Dorsen took the other, and sparking a flame on his fingertip, lit the plant to a smolder before re-covering it with the dome. The liquid inside the cylinder bubbled as both men took a deep drag from their mouthpieces. Alfred leaned back and blew out the smoke, instantly more relaxed than he had been in a long, long time. Dorsen seemed to mellow out a bit too, blowing a series of smoke rings from his lips before turning back to the conversation.

"I told you once before that you have great destinies to fulfill. I believe the time draws close, and *since* the time is close, I believe I'm going to tell you something my father advised against."

Alfred merely cocked an eyebrow at Dorsen as if inviting him to go-on.

"You're a god Alfred. Same as I, though not fathered or mothered by the same pair. Shame though, it'd have been awesome to have you as a brother. I suppose it's well enough we're friends though."

Alfred said nothing for a moment and Henry was still too absorbed in his video game to have been paying attention.

At last he replied, "You're high as shit man." The resolver threw his head back in a laugh before taking another draw from the tube.

Dorsen bellowed his chuckle before saying, "Well yeah, I most certainly am. But seriously Alfred, you're a bloody god. Not literally *bloody*, I've no idea what sort of god you are. But sure as I am high right now, you and I are two of a kind."

This time Alfred thought before saying anything. The way his wounds healed so quickly… the fact that the god Hashish hadn't been able to kill him and told him he wasn't human, and yet still… he didn't see how it was possible.

"Then why am I like *this*? If I'm a god like you say, why is it I can't change form like you and why do I live below, rather than in the heavens?"

"The answers to all of these questions- I'm not sure. As far as your body, that one is simple. Someone, an incredibly powerful one of our kind, has bound you to human flesh and sent you below the heavens. Who it was? I've no idea. Why they did it? I'm most positive now it has something to do with a destiny you're meant for. When I first met you I thought perhaps you were a half-god, a bastard son the result of some affair. But no, you have a god for a father and a goddess for a mother. I'm certain." Dorsen downed what was left of his drink, as if the long explanation had left him parched.

Once again Alfred grew lost in thought. He slurped down his gin and tonic, relishing the warmth of the alcohol mixing with the tingling in his brain from the Juzasaki.

At last he spoke, "I… I don't want to believe it because it sounds so ridiculous, but you've no reason to deceive me. And I *was* taken in as an infant by Jenni and Papari. They just found me one morning wrapped in blankets in the parking lot of the roller-rink."

"Believe me Al Moreno, my last intention is to deceive you. I wish I could do more to help you, to *free* you from the human body you're bound to, but I'm afraid only the one who sent you below can do that. Still, I can pour you a shot and give you the needed transportation to the signal on Thear. Better yet! I'll transport you to Silas Petrou himself, as he's wandered quite a ways from where his ship wrecked."

"Thank you Dorsen, f-for everything." Was all Al could think to say.

"Do not fear what you have learned today. It is something to be embraced, not to be wary of. Perhaps in due time you will learn more of your past and how you came to be the way you are. So… vodka?"

"Whiskey, double please." Alfred said before taking another toke from the smoke machine.

# CHAPTER SEVEN

Alfred had dragged a reluctant Henry away from Dorsen's collection of video games when it came time to go. The god had turned back into his preferred form of the raven and opened a swirling pathway that would teleport the pair to Silas Petrou. With one more word of thanks to Dorsen for telling him all that he had, a mildly drunk and quite high Alfred stepped into the portal with Henry in his pocket.

And although one would think a rift resolver would be used to inter-realm portals, Alfred hadn't entered one in a long time being in the state he was in now. Funny, he thought as he tried to ignore the swirling around him, I wonder if I'll still be intoxicated when we arrive. His question was answered a moment later as he toppled out of the portal's other end and landed on something soft that groaned as he hit it. Alfred groaned as well upon confirming he was still inebriated.

The thing beneath him began to move on its own accord. It was squishy with a firmness underneath and just as he opened his eyes, it threw Alfred from his place on top of it. It was a man.

"Where in the hell did you come from?" the man said in a noble voice.

Alfred halfway stumbled to his feet, setting Henry on the ground in case he needed assistance fighting whoever this was. Al studied him with a wary eye. Although his clothing was tattered and mud was strewn across his skin in many places, Al could tell he was one of those high-society chaps who was likely a spoiled brat growing up. He looked as if he were normally clean shaven, though a thin beard had appeared on his face and actually made him quite handsome. It matched his light brown hair and hazel eyes. His stature was best described as lithe- there was muscle in his arms yes, but he wasn't of the bulky sort. On his back Alfred could see there hung a bow, though the cannister for arrows was empty.

"Who-who are y-*you*?" Alfred slurred, throwing out an accusing index finger and pointing it at the man.

"My good man, are you *drunk*?" came the reply.

Alfred thought about that again for a minute. He took a quick tally of what all he had drank[19] before leaving Dorsen's cave.

---

[19] The gin and tonic, a shot of whiskey (double), and then some

"Yes." He said thoughtfully. Then added a second later, "And high."

"Well I must say I've never partaken in the Juza' myself, but dear sir where on this forsaken world did you find any alcohol? And if you'd be so kind as to point me in that direction." replied Silas Petrou.

The only part of that Alfred heard was 'never partaken in the Juza' and he felt quite sorry for the man. He began digging around in his coat pockets until he pulled out a small bag that was filled with crushed red leaves. Henry chirped from the ground, scanning a beam of golden light over the man.

"Alfred, this is Silas Petrou. The man we were sent to rescue!"

Both Al and Silas' eyes lit up at that.

"Oh *yaaa!* I forgot all about that. Wa-wassup Silas, the name's Moreno and this little bugger is Henry. I'm afraid I've lost our method of transportation home though. Well *I* can get home 'cuz I'm a god but I don't think y-you can travel to their realms so looks like we're stuck here Salmon... Simon, S-Silas."

"Haven't you got your blade on you? You must be from the Society then, if you were sent to retrieve me." the man ignored Al's talk of being a god,

---

creation Dorsen had insisted he take part in known as the "Soul Swirler." He wasn't positive, but pretty sure it was the last one that got him.

imagining it was merely a result of his intoxicated state.

"Ya but the damn thing won't work on this planet, 'less it's just to another place *on* the planet. Hey did you feel that?"

"*Ow,* fack!" Silas cursed, his accent really coming over the curse word.

Alfred laughed at how the man spoke, but Petrou didn't seem to notice. He was busy trying to cover himself from the acid rain that had started up again.

"C'mon man, I know a place we can get out from under this *stupid* rain." Al sliced the air in front of him with his rift blade and gestured for Silas to follow him through the newly created portal.

The man seemed in no position to disagree, so he followed Al through. Henry just managed to hop in before the rift closed. Now the three of them sat huddled under the structure Alfred had found earlier.

"I've really got to sober up. You don't mind if I-" Al glanced at the bag of leaves still in his hand. He had always been able to rely on the high of Juzasaki overtaking the drunkenness of alcohol.

"By all means do as you like. I just don't understand why your blade won't work here, it's incredibly strange. Then again, this whole *planet* is strange. That's why I was sent here to investigate originally."

Alfred had taken out one of two cigars he brought with him from Dorsen's cave. It was a shame really to waste even one of them, they were incredibly high quality, but were apparently what Dorsen used regularly to smoke Juza' out of. He tucked the spare one back in his jacket, saving it for Flux. They talked as he split the cigar and dumped out the tobacco inside, replacing it with the crushed red leaves and then going to work sealing it back up.

Night had by now begun to fall on the planet Thear. It was the time when its single moon hadn't risen high enough to provide any substantial light, so it was quite dark outside. Henry took the liberty to illuminate a soft golden glow where he sat in the center between the two resolvers.

"What exactly were you sent to investigate?"

"This acid rain, the vegetation in parts of the world that are decaying at an incredibly rapid rate- did you see those black spots on the planet's surface as you came in?"

Alfred thought back to looking out the viewing panel of their spaceship, there *had* been a lot of black areas. He held down his newly sealed cigar full of Juza' to Henry, who procured a little lighter from within his egg. Al took a deep drag as the little robot inverted the lighter back inside himself.

"Yeah, now that you mention it. And that's the decay?"

"Right. Which in itself isn't that odd. Worlds decay and die out all over the galaxies all the time. What's so strange is this world is dying at an alarming rate. Two weeks ago there was no acidic rainfall and those black spots wouldn't even have been viewable from space. And *now*, well you see."

Now that certainly was strange, Alfred thought. What could cause an entire planet to rapidly die when it was fine only a few weeks prior? Moreno could feel the high battling away his drunkenness and he was beginning to feel much better.

"What do you make of these ruins? And how come you don't have a rift blade yourself?"

"These ruins I believe come from a time long, long ago. They'd have to be, as there's been no intelligent life on this planet for millenniums. There likely aren't many species left here at all. But anyway, I don't have a rift blade. I wield a bow and use arrows with tips of rift. Only along with my ship, my stock of arrows has been lost." The man shot Alfred an amused look, as if he were surprised he didn't know he used a bow.

"And what happened to the ship?" Alfred asked, taking a few more pulls from the cigar before smashing it out on the stone floor beside him.

"It was one of the strangest things that'd ever happened to me. The ship's autopilot bit the dust as I was entering the atmosphere- which was fine. I simply took over the manual controls, but as I broke through the atmosphere my ship was suddenly surrounded by black clouds. Sensing something wretched was on its way, I sent out a distress signal. Sure enough, my left engine was struck by a bolt of wicked lighting and down I went. Had to use a bloody parachute! Never thought I'd use one of those outdated number. The sky had been clear until the instant I entered it." Petrou explained.

"That's extremely bizarre. You're right, this place *is* odd. I've gotten a strange feeling myself that it doesn't want me to leave. I had some companions, one a resolver, and he rifted them out of here just fine. And yet when I try to do the same- nothing. That reminds me, Henry can you begin broadcasting a signal in case Marcie and Aaron are trying to find us?"

"Of course s-"

*Grrrrrrr*

"What in Mother's Moons was *that*?" Petrou stood up quickly, Alfred doing the same.

## GRRRRRRR

"Henry shine a light over there, quick!"

Walking toward them from the other end of their shelter was a beast of some sort on its hind legs.

Henry's light couldn't reach quite far enough to make out exactly what it was. Then a flash of lightning lit up their surroundings, and standing between two of the stone pillars was something no one thought possible. It stood nine feet tall on its back legs, was covered in shaggy brown fur, and seemed to have an incredible mass about it. Another flash of lightning revealed two rows of razor-sharp teeth beneath its snout. Henry had gotten a good enough view to name the beast by what it was, however impossible it may have sounded.

"Alfred sir. That's a *bear!*"

# CHAPTER 8

"Bears have been extinct for thousands of years! How has one come to be on this damned planet of all places?" Petrou shouted over the raging acid and lightning storm.

"I've no idea! But it's coming towards us!" Alfred called back through the howling wind.

The bear was only a few yards in front of them now. With a wall to their back and the acidic rainfall taking away any chance of running for escape, Alfred couldn't think of what to do. For even if he were to open a rift back to where he found Silas, they'd still be under the wrath of the storm. And while Henry and himself might be fine against the stinging rain, the man he was sent to rescue could be hurt severely by the time they found any alternative shelter. Once again Al grew frustrated that his blade wasn't working properly.

"You've no choice but to slay the beast!" came Petrou's cry.

Though Al hated to admit it, fighting off the hulking animal might very well be their only chance. And being the only one equipped with a weapon, (however uncooperative it may be) he stepped forward. He didn't particularly want to fight the animal; bears were after all thought to have gone extinct thousands of years ago. This one seemed to be quite a formidable member of its species as well- the acid rain hadn't even been able to singe its fur, which kept its flesh safe from any real harm. Ah, the wonders of adaptation.

"Sir! You've no chance against that bear!" Henry yelled from his place on the ground.

"Thank you for the words of encouragement Henry. Just keep that light on so I can see."

Alfred drew his rift blade from its place at his belt, holding it before him in a readied stance. There was nothing but a few feet between him and the creature now. It dropped down on all fours and lumbered closer. Maybe he was just still incredibly high (he was) but he didn't think he saw malice in the animal's eyes. So, to the horror of both Silas Petrou and Henry the egg, Alfred did something only someone who had just smoked a lot of Juzasaki would do. He lowered his blade slowly to the ground, leaving it there, and then eased back up to his feet.

"Are you *facking* insane? Slay the beast, don't give it your weapon!" Petrou called hysterically, now filled with thoughts of why this man of all people had to be the one sent to retrieve him.

Moreno actually turned his back to the bear at this moment, offering it the perfect chance to attack, and lifted up one finger to his lips as if to tell Silas to shush. The bear did not lunge. When Alfred turned back to face it, it began doing a strange movement. First it looked directly at him, then it would swing its head over its shoulder. It would wait a moment and then do this again and again until at last Al thought he understood what it wanted. Being as high as he was, combined with the oddness of the world he seemed to be trapped on, Alfred did what he often does- left his fate to the will of the Universe.

"It wants me to follow it!" He shouted over his shoulder.

"It *wants* to facking eat you man! What exactly did you smoke!" Silas had now condemned his once-savior to pure insanity.

The bear performed its gesture one last time, then turned and slowly began to make its way back in the direction it had come from. Alfred started to follow, but Petrou and Henry both came forward to try and hold him back. The bear noticed this and quickly turned back around, bounding past Al and snarling at both Petrou and the little robot. Then it gazed at Alfred once more with its black eyes before carrying on.

"Henry, stay here with Silas. Keep that signal going out for Aaron and Marcie. I'll be okay, trust me."

Though the A.I. seemed a tad dismayed, it answered back faithfully, "I trust you sir."

"Even if the beast *has* befriended you, you'll get burned alive by this acid storm!" hollered Silas.

"I'll be fine, I'm a *fackin'* god. Or something like that." The resolver answered mostly to himself.

Alfred trudged on after the great furry mass, out between two of the stone pillars and into the windswept rainfall. In truth it did sting as it hit his skin, but as always the wound quickly repaired itself. He trailed a few feet behind the bear, who checked to make sure he was still following every so often. They went on through the ruins, pillars and cracked stone laying all over the ground around them. Remnants of old buildings were on both sides of him. It seemed as if the storm was picking up pace rather than showing any sign of relenting soon. Suddenly the bear took off in a great galloping run.

"Hey wait up! Where are you going?" Moreno yelled, his shout lost in the whipping winds.

Left without much of a choice, Alfred picked up the pace. Shielding his eyes from the worst of the storm, he ran blindly through the ruins in search of the guiding bear. But eventually he grew too weary to give chase any longer and bent over taking in deep breaths of air. A few drops of rain hit his tongue while his mouth was open, sizzling on its tender surface. Alfred looked up, a soft glow catching the corner of his eye.

It was green, a softer shade of the color, and he could just barely make it out through the darkness of the night. Logic was beginning to take over his mind where the Juza' had been prior. He should turn back. He had just followed an animal thought to be extinct, through an acidic rainstorm in the middle of the night, on a planet he was completely unfamiliar with. And yet something about the glow beckoned him. As if it were calling him. Singing a song meant only for his ears, a song that had been waiting to be sung for eons. So, with one last great breath to ease the fire in his lungs, he walked on toward the glow.

As he drew closer the light seemed to shine brighter. He found the ground beneath his feet was mushy and uneven from the beating it was taking in the storm. At last he approached the source of the green glow. It was a jewel- set in a crown upon the head of a statue of a woman. No, not a woman Alfred thought, a goddess. He wasn't positive how he knew for sure, but he was certain. The glow of the jewel at her head illuminated her features. There was something about her eyes that seemed to be almost alive.

Still feeling the strange sensation that he had been called to this place, Alfred reached out a hand toward the stone embezzled in her crown. His finger brushed it and the statue's eyes lit up in a flash of extraordinary green. The last thing he remembered seeing before his vision went black was that vivid color coming alive. Then a downward spiral, he felt as if the grass beneath his feet had gave way and he was freefalling. Down, down, down into the darkness.

**\*\*\* \*\*\* \*\*\***

"How much longer? I'm sick of this cramped cruiser." Marcie groaned.

"Well we just got into sector fifty-two and Thear is just outside fifty-three, so maybe another hour in this rust bucket. Can you believe Al used to drive this thing?"

"Well I suppose it's a vehicle. A kid should be happy to have anything that gives them the freedom to go where they please. I grew up on Hemphion Aaron, my first taste of freedom was riding an old motorbike through the forests."

"That doesn't sound so ba-"

"Through the forests where I would kill small animals to sustain my village as I avoided being eaten by the larger ones."

"Right. Pretty terrible, got it." Flux finished.

"You didn't know Alfred when he drove this thing? I thought you two went to school together?" Marcie changed the subject.

"No, I went to the *academy*[20] at the same time as Alfred. Well actually he couldn't enroll until a year after me, but the bastard still ended up getting his blade[21] before I did."

"What was he like back then?" Marcie wondered aloud.

"Curious about the background of the father-to-be, eh?" Aaron gave her a smirk.

"Is that so bad? I mean, I love him and everything... I just don't know a whole lot about his past."

"Well, that's probably because he doesn't either. Poor kid was found in a roller-rink parking lot wrapped in tattered blankets. He's lucky some intergalactic scum didn't find him and eat him before

---

[20] The academy is where acolytes train to become full-fledged rift resolvers.

[21] An acolyte "getting his or her blade" is an equivalent term to graduating. One receives their weapon upon graduating the academy. As you've come to see, not all resolvers choose to wield a blade- as there are other variations of rift weaponry to choose from.

Papari came outside and heard the little bastard crying."

Marcie seemed more thoughtful now saying, "Yeah. It must be hard not to know where you're from or why you were abandoned."

"But anyway, Moreno was pretty much like you'd expect while we were in the academy. Star pupil, handsome young buck- the ladies there were obsessed with him of course." Marcie shot him a scowl upon hearing the last part.

"Oh c'mon now, you asked! Al never payed them any mind anyway. Always too obsessed with being the best, no time for any distractions. Except Juzasaki- that man loved to smoke. Think it helped him relax after training, probably helped keep his mind off those questions of why he'd been abandoned and all that too. But rest assured *Marceline*, he's a truly wonderful guy. Not to toot his horn too much, but I know he'll make a great father."

Marcie ignored the part where Flux had used her full name, "That's sweet of you Aaron, thank you."

One of the monitors on the spacecruiser's dash was emitting a little ping every few seconds now.

"What's that?" Marcie asked.

Flux turned back to face the monitor, examining the details of the blipping noise. He looked as if he were reading something that appeared when he clicked on the blip.

Turning back around he exclaimed, "It's a signal from Henry with his coordinates on Thear! And a message is attached. It reads:

Found Petrou. In ruins. Not Silas he's fine, we're literally in some ruins. Alfred went chasing after a bear, please hurry back."

# CHAPTER NINE

Alfred slowly blinked open his eyes, the cold black he had slipped into instantly replaced with bright sunshine. He felt as if he had just slept the night through in the most comfortable bed and yet now he saw that it was grass he was laying on. Getting to his feet, he got a better sense of his surroundings. What he saw took his breath away.

A meadow of flowers, no he realized, not just flowers. There seemed to be a representative from each of a million or more species of plants. Trees, vegetables, and exotic fruits popped up everywhere in a bountiful harvest. Each appeared to have reached peak ripeness. Then the creatures began to appear. Alfred spotted the bear that he had followed to the statue; it looked at him for a moment before wandering off through one of several gardens. Next he saw a group of four-legged woodland animals. The one in the lead had a stick-like form protruding from its forehead, and Al found that he somehow knew this meant the creature was a male. This couldn't be the same decrepit planet he was on before, could it?

He walked forward, that same sensation that had drawn him ever closer to the statue once again working its magic. He gazed up in wonder as he passed through an arched passage of beautiful red folded flowers, then across a quiet pebble-ridden stream. And at last he saw her, beneath a colossal tree sat the goddess in the statue on a throne of interwoven branches.

With a welcoming wave of her hand she beckoned him forward. He walked on without hesitation, as if he were in a trance. But no, he was still aware of any danger that might be around him. It just seemed as if there was nothing to fear, as if this place he had found himself in was too pure to cause any harm. A part of him felt like this was home but he wasn't sure how. At last he had come to her, where she sat comfortably in the chair beneath the tree. Though it was made of solid branch, Al noticed it was covered in a soft moss that must have been meant for cushioning.

She smiled at him. It sent all the warmth of a thousand suns into his chest. As he looked upon her, he realized she didn't appear to be any older than eighteen. But her eyes told that she was ageless, that there had been a seemingly infinite amount of time in her existence. Her blonde hair flowed elegantly down to her waist. Atop her head was the same crown the statue had worn, the same one that had brought Alfred to this mysterious and wonderful place. Her dress was as if spiders had handcrafted it of silk then dyed it green in some variety of the endless plants around them. She was beautiful.

"Hello. I've waited a long time to see you." She said, her voice as gentle as the smoothest tide caressing the sand along a foreign coast.

"You've been waiting for me?" he asked. No surprise in his voice, just the need for confirmation.

"Yes. I haven't seen you since you were a babe." She replied.

It felt too strangely right, once she said that he had to ask, "Are you…?" there was almost a tinge of hopefulness that could be heard in the question.

She laughed softly before answering. "Not exactly. I'm only your mother in the sense that part of you is human, and here you are on the world where humankind began. I am this world. Perhaps it would clear things up if I introduced myself."

"Yes, perhaps." Alfred looked at her, curiosity burning in his eyes.

"Some once knew me as Mother Earth, though in the heavens I am Gaea. In more recent times my world has come to be called Thear, humorous in a way that it should be an anagram of the original name. Then again, Chaos *is* known to be a fan of comedy."

"It's nice to meet you. There has long been a great debate among the galaxies where the human race first began. I'm honored to be able to visit." Alfred said respectfully.

Gaea shook her head as she stood from her throne. The way the sunlight shone through her hair, there was something so naturally beautiful about her.

"Not an unintentional visit. You were destined. I was there the day they had to give you up, or *down* I should say. A newborn, tossed below the heavens and bound to the flesh that makes my presence feel like home to you. It's a terrible thing, truly. But I knew… I knew one day you were meant to save me."

"You know my parents then, if you were there the day I was sent below. You *have* to know my parents." There was an excitement that couldn't be hidden in his voice.

"I do."

"Then tell me! Please, I've wondered for so long. I've just recently learned what I really am and I don't understand it at all. But to know, just to *know* would be… something." He pleaded her. Mother Earth could see the desperation in his eyes. The questions he had long kept hidden in the back of his mind now coming to life as he spoke them here in this sacred place.

"I'm afraid I can't do that. Not until you do me a favor." She looked away, as if it sorrowed her to hold his truth ransom.

She was surprised when he said nothing of the unfairness in her deal but instead replied a simple, "Anything."

She turned back, stepping closer to him until the goddess was so near there couldn't have been more than a foot between them.

"Save me. Thear is dying and with it so am I."

"How?"

"You must triumph over the depraved souls that have taken root in my earth. They eat away at me, bringing their caustic storms and plague to this planet."

"Souls?" Alfred asked.

Though the quest appeared to have been thrown on him in a heartbeat, if it meant a way to learn about his past he would do it without question.

"Yes. They are the Nosoi[22], spirits of sickness and plague who have made their sinister home in my earth."

---

[22] Daemons escaped from Pandora's Jar. Yes, *jar*, not box- look it up.

Alfred, using the tactical part of his brain that made him a skilled resolver, continued his questioning. "How many are their number?"

"There are many Nosoi, far too many to number. Here, however, there are four. These are the spirits that have long plagued men with misery, misfortune, sickness, death, and the like. But this matters not, for only one need be defeated for the rest to follow suit. *Phthisis.*"

"Fine. I'd be glad to help even if you knew nothing of my parents. I might have recently learned that I come from different realms, but I've lived my life so far as a human. I'd be honored to defend the planet on which the human race began."

"I am gratified by your enthusiasm. It seems the Moroi know the matters of fate well indeed. Though you fight for the chance of new beginnings in humankind, this is a battle you must endure with your strength as a god."

That made sense enough to Al, fighting daemons = using his power as a god. Simple enough.

"Where do I find him, this Phthisis?"

"I'm afraid the journey is nearly as perilous as the duel you are to encounter upon your arrival. It is good that your friends are making their way back, you will need their help on this quest to save Thear." Alfred's eyes sparked at the mention of his friends, but he kept silent as Gaea went on. "You will have to journey within the crust of my world, nearly to the center, as this is where the Nosoi have rooted and where Phthisis sits on a throne of rot. Laughing as he watches me crumble into the infection he spreads. Your companions can help get you there, but once you arrive those that were born below will not be able to enter the gateway."

Alfred bowed to the beautiful woman before looking up at her slowly from on his knee. "I won't let you down."

She smiled, bringing that instant happiness to him once more. That sense of belonging, the one he had always seemed to misplace in life. Journeying from one sector of the universe to the next in pursuit of Society missions. Gaea leaned down and lay a gentle kiss on his forehead.

"Return me to life, dearest Lýsi." She whispered softly.

Alfred looked into her eyes as the vision faded away, the lush green around him slowly disappearing into black once more. And as he felt himself returning to a place that seemed far below where he had walked in the meadow of a million flowers, he thought of another girl with emerald green eyes. A girl who would be waiting for him when he woke.

# CHAPTER TEN

Alfred opened his eyes to a pair staring right back at him. For a heartbeat he thought it was Marcie, but no- soon his brain processed the masculine features of the face around the eyes that blinked at him.

"Are you alright man? You had the largest smile on your face as you lay there twitching below this relic all night." Silas Petrou pointed to the statue before continuing. "Looked so damn happy I didn't have it in me to disturb you, so I waited until the morning before I woke you up."

Al got to his feet with a hand from Silas saying, "I'm fine, thanks."

"By the way, your egg went blasting off into that forest of firs last night. Said something about some people coming. He got really excited and zipped away."

Suddenly a loud crash sounded from the nearby forest Silas had just mentioned.

"It must be Marcie and Aaron, perhaps they're following Henry's signal and that's why he's gone off to meet them. But that noise, I better make sure they're not in any trouble. You coming?"

Silas seemed to notice something different about the resolver now. The authority was now clear in his voice. The man nodded, of course he would accompany a fellow member of the Society, especially if it brought him closer to getting off this damned planet!

The two of them ran off through the ruins until they reached the first trees that marked entry to the woodland. As they made their way through the trees the crash sounded again. Al redirected them to head in the direction of the noise. A few minutes later they heard it once more, but this time it seemed much closer. Suddenly something scurried across the ground in front of them, skidding to a halt once it noticed the two men.

"Henry!" Alfred exclaimed, quickly recognizing the egg.

"Alfred, you've got to come fast. Marcie and Aaron are trapped by some terrible looking monster. Hurry, follow me!" the A.I. explained quickly before zipping back down the trail in front of them.

With a quick nod to Silas, Alfred led the way after Henry. He found himself half-tripping over roots and ducking under stray branches. It seemed Henry wasn't paying much attention to whether the path he was taking was the most suitable for the two men to follow after. However, it wasn't much farther before they broke out of a patch of brush and into a large clearing. Here Alfred and Silas witnessed what was making the crash noise.

The fir trees made up half of the clearing's circular boundary. But the side of the clearing opposite of the men was fenced off by tall, massive rocks. The kind that likely couldn't be climbed without proper equipment. Tucked in a corner behind two boulders, Alfred could just make out Aaron and Marcie's heads. Pinning them there was the monster that Henry had mentioned.

On its four legs the animal stood around twelve feet tall. Its coat looked to be comprised of shaggy fur, though it was ragged and its hair had fallen out in many places. The crashing was coming from the ginormous set of curled horns atop its head. It was obviously quite frustrated at not being able to reach Marcie and Aaron and so every few minutes it would back up and charge in the direction of where they hid. The rock wall that trapped them from behind was rammed[23] violently by the creature. As its horns made contact it caused bits of rock to break off and fall

---

[23] Get it?

onto Alfred's companions. Without putting much thought into any sort of a rescue plan, Alfred proceeded to yell out to the great beast.

"Hey you horny[24] bastard, leave my woman alone!" he shouted out across the clearing. Then a moment later added, "And Flux too I guess!"

The hulking animal swung its head around, revealing a gruesome face to Silas and Al. Its wide eyes dripped green pus and even nastier substances were oozing from its nostrils. The whole clearing smelled like mange and decay.

Alfred approached the monster, raising his rift blade in his right hand. It studied him for a moment through its obviously disease-ridden eyes. Then, lowering its head down so that its mighty horns faced frontwards, it pawed at the ground with one of its forelegs as if preparing to charge.

"Alfred get out of the way!" Marcie called from behind the boulders.

But the monster was already charging forward at the two men and the little robot. Henry scooted to the right side of the beast and Silas rolled away to the left. Al stood still, studying the pace at which the muscular legs were switching places in order to carry the animal forward. Then, in one great ducking motion, he leaned back with the tip of his blade held

---

[24] Come on, *that* was a good one.

firm in place. The animal went right over him, Alfred balanced precariously between all four of its hooves as they pounded by. A large abscess was now strung across the length of the monster's stomach. Alfred ran a little to distance himself from the brute.

"My good man. What a move indeed!" Silas offered his praise from where he now stood by Marcie, Aaron, and Henry.

Aaron and Marcie had taken the opportunity to escape from their cornered position against the rocks. Now she embraced Alfred, but he was forced to let her go quickly for the monster had turned back around. They could see a great mass of septic entrails on the ground beside it, obviously released by Al's sweeping cut. The beast shuddered in pain, swinging its head around and trying to lick at the wound with its swollen black-spotted tongue.

"Would either of the two of you happen to be rift resolvers?" Silas asked.

Flux hadn't payed much attention to the man who had come with Alfred, for he had been focused on the beast. But upon hearing his voice he turned and made the realization of who Silas was.

"Y-You're Silas Petrou! The grand bow master, the king of arrows, the-" Aaron was interrupted by Marcie.

"Really Aaron, right now? The doofus here is a resolver, as well as a big fan of yours if you couldn't tell. Oh shit! Watch out everyone!" Marcie shouted a quick warning at the end, causing everyone to look up in panic.

The mutant animal had begun to charge again, seemingly much faster now from the rage of being injured.

"Your rift blade for a moment, if you don't mind?" Silas remained in place beside Flux, while Marcie and Alfred dove back over the rocks she had been hiding behind before.

"I'd be honored!" Flux pulled his rift gun from its holster, shooting open a portal beside him before tossing the weapon to Petrou.

Aaron leaped into the swirling vortex and Silas just managed to dive out of the way after catching the weapon. The beast rammed into the rock wall behind Marcie and Al once again, causing the ground around them to shake violently. Then, yanking one of its horns out of the rock, it started to back up a few paces as if preparing to charge again. Alfred felt something heavy fall on his back, thinking at first some rock had collapsed when the animal struck. He quickly realized it was Flux.

"Of all the places, you rifted here?" Al exclaimed.

"Hey, you cornered yourself too!" Aaron shot back.

"Where'd Simon go?" Marcie asked, peeking up from behind the rock as if looking for the man's trampled body.

"*Silas*. His name is *Silas*." Aaron corrected.

"Not sure," Alfred began, "but I don't think these boulders are going to hold much longer." The rocks in front of them now had several cracks, likely from the beast's earlier attempts at getting Marcie and Flux.

The mutated animal was pawing especially hard at the ground now. It seemed enraged that it had been foiled once again by its prey. As it thundered forward at them, Marcie slung a sword out of its place in her armor while Alfred readied himself with his blade once more. Aaron, now weaponless, cowered behind the soon-to-be-demolished rocks. Things were not looking good for the three of them. As it neared the half-way point to the boulders, a high-pitched mechanical voice blared from on top of the rock wall above them.

"Announcing the Archduke[25] of Archery, Silas Petrou!" it was Henry, perched beside the rift resolver.

Suddenly the monster looked up, skidding its charge to a halt at the sound of Henry's voice. Marcie,

---

[25] Not really an Archduke. Just really good at- well you get it.

Aaron, and Alfred looked up to see the man with an arrow drawn back in the string of his bow. The tip of it glistened with a bright purple glow. Without a word Silas released the arrow, sending it soaring through the air in a direct line to where it thudded into the animal's chest. The beast stumbled back a half-step, but only a second later another arrow tip punctured beside it. Then another, and another. Alfred saw Petrou's hands as a mere blur as they pulled and shot ammunition from the now full cannister on his back. Within twenty seconds there were eight arrows stuck in the monster's chest, forming a near perfect outline of an octagon. The animal had fallen onto its front knees now, but appeared as if it were about to make the effort to stand up. That's when the final arrow struck, dead center in the octagon.

A bright purple glow emitted from each shaft, before an explosion rippled through the entire length of the beast's body. The blast maintained the shape of the octagon all the way through, leaving behind a tunnel of gore and blood. Its head lolled to the side and it collapsed, causing the clearing to shake one last time. Silas pulled back another arrow, sticking it in the ground before him, then shot one more below. Henry leaped into the rift he formed and soon they were both beside the others. Silas handed Aaron back his gun.

"That was *incredible!*" Flux cheered, tucking it back into his holster.

"Well I managed to grab some rift arrows real quick from the sector twelve headquarters. So, you guys ready to complete this rescue mission and head on back or what?" Petrou responded.

"About that..." Alfred shot the man a sympathetic look.

# CHAPTER ELEVEN

"Damn, I haven't seen this thing in years. I figured Papari would have had it junked by now." Alfred said as he looked at the spacecruiser he used to drive as a teenager.

"The flames are a… most interesting touch." Silas commented.

"Well she's all yours to fly back, or you can just rift. But I can't leave here yet even if I wanted to. I just don't think Thear would allow it." Al explained.

Silas looked at the cruiser for a minute, then turned his gaze back to Alfred and the others.

"It was my mission to investigate the nature of all the decay and madness on this backwater planet. And it seems you're tied into figuring that out." Petrou paused as if thinking over his decision for another moment. "I'll be glad to accompany you and your crew."

Aaron nudged Marcie with his arm and spoke in a giddy voice to her, "He's *so* honorable."

She rolled her eyes and positioned herself closer to Alfred. "So, you said we have to go near the planet's core, but how do we get there? And how are we going to survive the increase in temperature? And *how* do you know all this anyway?"

Now Henry interjected. "He followed after a bear and was transported to the realm of the goddess of this planet, right Alfred? And she told you all about how humanity began on Thear and how you're a go-"

"How I'm a *go*ing to save the planet from some rotten spirits known as the Nosoi who have taken root near the core." Al finished for the robot, not quite ready to explain to Marcie that he had recently discovered he was a god.

She shot him an odd glance but said nothing. Flux, who was intently staring at Silas' bow, looked away for a second to ask, "So how do we get there?"

"Taking a scan of the planet's heat map, I've located the entry point that can carry us the farthest toward the center as possible. However, unless you all feel like two weeks of hiking, I recommend we take the spacecruiser." Henry answered.

"You've got to be kidding, there's no way we're all going to fit in there." Marcie complained.

Twenty minutes later they were all crammed into Alfred's old spacecruiser. Lucky for them it was only a two-hour flight, but even that was enough to have everyone ready to get out as soon as Henry successfully landed them. They enthusiastically exited the cruiser on a small plateau surrounded by rocky terrain. Henry led the way onwards through the rocks with Silas and Aaron behind him and Alfred and Marcie taking up the rear. Every so often they'd have to climb over rocks; when this happened Henry simply released a propeller out of the top of his egg and hovered over them. After a while the rocks lessened and the ground beneath their feet gradually sloped down.

"Did you really shoot an arrow into a target three miles aw-" Marcie overheard Flux chatting to Silas in front of her before she tuned him out.

"You're okay right? I mean, it just seems like something's kind of bothering you and I was really worried when we got separated." Al asked as he walked in pace with her.

That caught her a bit off guard. "I'm okay, I was worried about you too. I kind of thought something might be troubling *you*, actually."

Alfred turned and looked at her for a second. "Well I… I have to tell you something. Something really crazy that I had a hard time believing at first, but now it just seems like it *has* to be the truth."

Marcie perked up at that. "I have something I need to tell you too! But go ahead, you first." She was getting excited and a little nervous now. This could be the perfect opportunity to break the news.

"When I visited the realm of Gaea, she… well she told me that she knows my parents." He got out at last.

"Baby, that's great!" she paused for a moment, not sure of his reaction. "I mean, that is *good* news, right?"

He answered quickly, "Yeah, yeah! It's just that there's a little more to it than that. She uh, she told me that my parents are gods. Well, my dad is a god and my mother would obviously be-"

Marcie's mind had just realized two things, one directly after the other. 'Y-you're a god? But that means the ba-"

"We've arrived everyone! The entry point to Thear's core is *right* here!" Henry sang out loudly, bringing everyone else's conversations to a standstill.

"We can talk more about it soon, and I definitely want to hear whatever you have to tell me babe, just gotta-"

"Yeah, yeah it's fine!" she answered back fast as he made his way up to the front of the group.

Alfred found himself looking down into a cave opening. Picking Henry up as the A.I. illuminated the way in front of them, he beckoned the others to follow. There was a good six feet from one side of rock to the other and the roof of the underground tunnel was around ten inches higher than Alfred's head. The group had taken up a similar formation as when they were above ground- only now Marcie, Al and Henry were in the lead. Marcie considered bringing up their conversation from before, but there would be no privacy in the quietness of the tunnel.

Al stumbled, suddenly blinded by something silky in his eye. Quickly he ran a hand across his eyelids, gathering up a kind of string-like substance.

"What is this stuff?" he asked as he wiped it across his pants. Looking around he noticed there were great swaths of the silky strings stretching[26] across the tunnel walls ahead.

Henry flashed his light over a few patches of the stuff. "My scans inform me these are the product of a species. What species that is, I am uncertain."

Al pulled out his blade and took up the lead again, cutting through the web-like strings to form a path for the others. As they continued on it was harder and harder for the group to tell how much time had passed. At some points the path sloped down so much they had to stand four across and all connect arms, the person on each end bracing the group against the walls as they stepped in time. Eventually Al decided a break would be good for everyone.

---

[26] Talk about an alliteration!

They sat against the rock wall on either side, Henry taking up the middle between them and illuminating their surroundings in a soft amber glow.

"One thing's for sure, it's definitely gotten a tad warmer since we first started down." Silas called out to no one in particular.

"That doesn't make much sense though." Al started, "We're still days away from being anywhere close enough to where there should be a noticeable temperature increase."

Henry joined the conversation, "Though you are correct Alfred, there *shouldn't* be any significant increase at this stage of the journey, my sensors indicate that it actually is a few degrees hotter than where we entered."

"It's probably something to do with those rotten spirits you were talking about, the Nosy or whatever." Aaron reasoned.

"Regardless, we've got to keep going. C'mon, let's go a bit further before we stop for a longer rest." This time Marcie spoke up, and Al nodded in agreement to her as he got to his feet.

The next few days of travel through the tunnels was quite mundane. Two things were certain- they were going deeper into Thear and the temperature was rising. Other than that, the only problems that arose were food and water. These were quickly solved by Aaron and Silas, who rifted to their headquarters and raided the supplies when needed. Alfred's blade still refused to open a rift off the world of Thear. He even tried stepping into one of Flux's that led to Jenni's Roller-Rink, and yet Al simply passed right through it as if nothing were there. Thear really must have needed him to stay put.

On the morning[27] of the third day in the tunnels, the heat had gotten to be almost unbearable. Marcie was better off than Aaron and Silas, her armor helped keep her body temperature regulated at normal levels. Al had noticed it was warmer, but wasn't feeling the increase like the others were. It didn't seem as if the other two men were going to be able to go on much longer. They could only rift somewhere and cool down for very brief periods of times, otherwise they'd fall behind and get lost. A resolver can only rift somewhere he's been before after all, and without Henry's directions they'd likely get lost when the tunnel came to one of the many splits they had already encountered.

As night came on that day they lay stretched out on the rocky floor, the only one who had managed to fall asleep through the heat was Flux.

---

[27] They would have had no way of knowing it was morning, but Henry woke them with a charming alarm each new day.

"Henry turn that light off will ya? You're giving my brain the illusion its hotter than it already is." Alfred whispered to the egg.

"I don't have any lights on sir. I turned them off promptly when Miss Marcie threatened to chuck me against the cave wall."

That got Alfred to sit upright, a bit bewildered and beginning to believe he might be hallucinating. But the A.I. was right, he had no lights shining from his metal egg. Still, he noticed, there was a soft glow that seemed to be coming from just around the next bend in the tunnel. They must not have noticed it when they first reached the area because Henry's light had been on. Quickly Al gathered the others, and he led the way around the bend in the tunnel. He soon found the source of the light. It was a strange kind of rock he had never seen before that was chunked in various sections of the walls. It emitted a warm red iridescence and as they ran on down the path it grew more frequent. Along with more of the strange rock, there also seemed to be a greater abundance of the sticky strings.

Al had gotten a little way ahead of the others in his growing excitement. We've got to be close, he thought to himself, these rocks *must* mean that we're close. The heat was blistering now, but Al took no notice. The glowing rocks had come to make up the cave walls entirely, casting their brilliant light all around him. Finally the path opened into a great cavern made of the stuff, and for a moment Alfred thought he might have been wrong about being close to whatever he was trying to find. But then he saw it.

One section of the cavern wall wasn't made up of the red rock, it was a near perfect circle eight feet in diameter and carved from black stone. As Al approached it he saw there were words printed on its surface. Marcie and the others had caught up now, and she read the words once to herself before saying them aloud.

"It runs around a city but never moves. What is it?" she read to the others.

"Ooo, a riddle!" Sang out Henry, "I love riddles!"

# CHAPTER TWELVE

"Well go-ahead Henry, solve it. This has to be something to do with the Nosoi." Al prompted his robotic friend.

"Searching. Computing." The little egg chirped.

"Henry why are you saying that stuff? You've literally never done that before." Aaron panted from behind, still feeling the worst of the heat around them.

"I thought it'd make it seem like this riddle took me more than .017 seconds to solve." The A.I. explained cheerfully then added, "The answer is a Wall. A wall runs around a city but never moves."

The words that had previously been written on the stone slowly faded. Then a new script of words flashed in their place.

*No cheating permitted. The soul-less may not answer.*

"What! That's some bullshit." Aaron commented.

A second later the words on the rock changed again.

*Living without breath,*
*Cold as water, cold as death.*
*Clad in mail that never clinks,*
*Never thirsts but always drinks?*

"Hmm, I must say I always did enjoy a good riddle as a young lad. Give me a moment to think somewhere a bit cooler on it." Petrou offered.

"Sure, go ahead. We'll be here." Al replied, and the man opened a rift to somewhere where he could think without the heat.

Aaron followed Silas into the Rift, likely from both wanting to stay near the man and to cool down himself.

"Clad in mail that never clinks, never thirsts but always-" Al was saying to himself when Henry lit up suddenly with an excited chirp.

"It's a *fish!*"

The words dissolved once more, revealing the same "no cheating permitted" inscription again.

"Damn it Henry, you *aren't* allowed to answer." Alfred reminded the robot.

"I'm sor-" Henry was interrupted by a rift opening near the black part of the wall.

Out came Silas who shouted in an excited manner as he landed on his two feet. "I've got it! It's a *fish!*"

Marcie groaned, Alfred simply shook his head before looking back to see what the next riddle was.

### What question may you never with honesty give the answer "Yes."?

"What did I miss? Oh for Saturn's sake, did the bloody robot answer again?" Petrou sighed as he saw Alfred nod yes.

"Henry, *please* keep quiet this time." Al stressed.

"Oh don't be so harsh on him, maybe he can give us clues without saying the actual answer." Marcie suggested.

"Didn't you threaten to slam the robot into a cave wall not so long ago?" Silas mused.

Before she could reply the cave wall revealed another line of script beneath the riddle. There were only two words.

### No. Clues.

"Well it was a nice thought honey." Al put his arm around her affectionately.

Time dragged on as the group sought to think of the answer to the riddle without Henry's help. Marcie, Aaron, and Silas took turns going in out of rifts to cool down. Alfred was stuck in the thick heat of the cavern, but it really wasn't bothering him a whole lot[28]. He tried to think of questions that couldn't honestly be answered with yes, but it seemed like he would find one and then think of a scenario where it didn't work. At some point he fell asleep with his head resting against the black stone.

About ten minutes later Aaron emerged from a rift back into the cave. He looked as if he had just taken a cool shower, though it could have just been sweat from re-entering the hot zone. Marcie and Silas were both resting. Petrou at the sector twelve headquarters and Marcie at the roller-rink. Flux noticed Al laying up against the side of the wall, and he felt bad that his friend couldn't leave like the rest of them.

"Hey Al, are you asleep?" he called out to the resolver.

Two things happened almost simultaneously then.

Henry cheered loudly, "You got it Aaron sir!"

The circle of black stone against the red walls of the cavern began to open from the middle. Each half of the circle slowly began to move into the red beside

---

[28] Whenever he started to feel the slightest bit warm, he reminded himself of when the god Hashish scorched him with ridiculous heat. The temperature of the cave paled in comparison.

it. This stirred Alfred and he got to his feet upon feeling his headrest move. He stood beside Henry and Aaron, watching as a revolving vortex of shimmering scarlet color appeared in place of the black stone. It was a portal of some kind if Moreno had ever seen one[29].

Henry called out again with delight, this time to Alfred. "Mr. Flux got it Alfred! What question may you never honestly answer with yes? *Are you asleep*?"

"Wow would ya look at that. I solved the riddle." Aaron flashed a grin.

"You were the last one I would have guessed would find the answer, but I give you credit pal- you got it." Alfred smiled back, realizing in the back of his head that his companion had only answered correctly by accident.

Oh well, he thought, better to let him have his moments. "Hey smart-guy, why don't you go get Petrou and Marcie and let them know we figured it out."

Flux nodded at Alfred's command, exiting through a rift and reappearing a few minutes later with both Marcie and Silas following after. There was an awkward silence among all of them before Alfred finally spoke.

---

[29] He might've seen a few in his day.

"I know it's been a grueling and taxing few days traveling through the tunnels. I want you all to know how much I appreciate you coming with me and helping me get this far. But now I've got to go on alone, well other than Henry, for the goddess told me the rest of you won't be able to enter the gateway."

"I was happy to help a fellow resolver, and thank *you* for finding me. I admit I thought you were a bit mad when you went chasing off after that bear, but you're a good man Moreno. Best of luck in there." Silas answered first.

"Stay safe Al. Henry, watch out for him." Aaron gave his friend a pat on the back as he finished.

The other two resolvers turned their attention away for a minute as Marcie moved closer to embrace Al.

"I love you. Be careful in there." She said to him.

"I love you too. I'll be okay, I know we've still got some things to talk about when I get back."

She smiled warmly at him before giving him a quick kiss. Then she was on her way over to stand next to Aaron.

"We'll be waiting for you outside, near the entrance to the tunnel." Flux reminded him.

"I'll see you there."

With one last look at Marcie, Alfred scooped up Henry and stepped into the swirling gateway.

Marcie smiled to herself as she watched him disappear into the colorful portal. She was confident in Al. He would be alright. He *had* to come back alright.

"Well I'll be seeing you two, or perhaps not. Whatever the Universe intends, I suppose." Silas said kindly to Marcie and Aaron. "It was a plea-"

He was interrupted as a great length of string came out of nowhere and wrapped around his legs and torso. Petrou fell to the floor with a thud, struggling against the silky substance that now entwined him.

"What th-" Aaron started to shout, but he too was soon absorbed in the sticky strings.

Marcie's assassin instincts kicked in, and she managed to cartwheel to the side before the blast of web that was meant for her could make contact. Turning around and drawing a shortened scimitar from her armor, she saw what had been creating the webs they had encountered throughout their days traveling the tunnels.

"Oh shit." Her mouth opened wide as she took in the sight of the horror.

"Oh *shit*." Both Aaron and Silas echoed from where they lay restrained on the cavern floor.

# CHAPTER THIRTEEN

Alfred felt the terrible rush of vertigo slam into his head as hard as the cave walls he had been surrounded by before. Now all around him there was nothing but scarlet color with silver lines mixed in.

"Sir, are you alright? Look Alfred, I've taken up my wolf form again." Henry shouted, his voice coming across the swirling colors like waves crashing into Alfred's ears.

Slowly he turned and looked beside him. His perception was off inside the portal, it seemed as if Henry was both very close to him and yet also incredibly far away. But sure enough, the A.I. was no longer contained in his little egg. Across the portal ran a golden wolf[30], stretching out longer in length than Alfred's full height.

"Lookin' good buddy. Hey, are we almost there?" the resolver asked his partner.

"Get on my back sir, I'll get us the rest of the way through much faster."

Alfred began forcing himself over to Henry, almost feeling like he might get sick as the image of the wolf continuously moved closer and then farther away from him. But at last his outstretched hands found the feel of fur and he was able to situate himself on Henry's back. Suddenly his headache and nausea faded and his perception somewhat regulated. Just like the very first time he traveled with Henry to Gosia's realm, being in contact with the A.I. really made Al feel better.

He watched the colors go by him faster and faster as Henry bounded down the length of the vortex. After a period that Al could neither describe as long nor short, the wolf gave one terrific leap and he found himself on the other side of the portal.

Henry was still beside him and in wolf form. But now Alfred found himself on a great sweeping cliff of obsidian rock. It was black all the way through and yet somehow shimmered with a faint purple. Ahead

---

[30] This is Henry's preferred form when traveling to strange realms with Alfred. Henry the wolf returns!

of him lay a path marked by lit torches sticking up on either side all the way to the cliff's edge- here there appeared to be a structure of some kind. Turning around Alfred expected to see the scarlet portal, but instead the purple-black ground merely stretched on and on farther than his eyes could reach.

"Well I guess we know which way to go." He half-joked to the A.I.

They walked side by side through the rows of torches that were cemented into the black they strolled on. It didn't take them long to reach the structure at the cliff's edge. Al could now tell that it was a gate. Suddenly three lengths of individual light rose up from the ground in front of the gate. The lights quickly took shape into three of the ugliest beings Alfred had ever laid eyes on.

"We are the Nos-" the bulkiest one began, he stood in the middle.

"Jesus on Jupiter, what in starlight is that smell?" Al interrupted the spirit as he gagged on the rotten stench flowing from the three of them.

"You were saying?" Henry, trying to be polite as always, voiced from beside him.

The spirit glanced at the wolf with a look of mild curiosity before starting up once more.

"We are the Nosoi. I am Deacon, this is Tyraine, and that's Alcina." He indicated first to himself and then to the male and female spirits beside him.

Alfred finally managed to get his coughing and gagging under control and now looked upon the nasty things before him. The middle one, Deacon, was an absolutely wretched looking character. He had the face of a man but it was disfigured horribly. His gnarled teeth actually ripped through his cheek in places, opening a porthole view into the dreadful insides of his mouth. His body was best described as lumpy and the skin that stretched over it carried a green tinge. Deacon, as well as Tyraine, wore white togas that stretched over their gruesome figures.

Tyraine was much leaner than his brother and stood close to eight feet tall. His skin was a similar color to Deacon's but his torso was incredibly thin. Al had to angle his neck up to see the spirit's wart-ridden face. Finally, he looked to the female spirit.

Rather than a toga, she was wearing a white dress that actually fit her quite well. Her face appeared normal enough, if one could get past the horrid shade of vomit-green that her skin was comprised of. Her hair was at most a dozen strands of grease-ridden gray. She smiled and her face creased and crumpled in the most ill-fitting way.

"Tyraine, Alcina, and Deacon. I think I'll call you Filthy, Foul, and…" Al paused a moment as he looked to name Deacon last. He pointed at him, finishing "And you- well you just look *fucked*."

"You joke now Lýsi, but just wait 'til you see what we have in store for you." Deacon garbled.

"The name's Al." he corrected the spirit.

"You have much to learn today. If you can survive that is." Tyraine snickered.

"Where is Phthisis, your leader?" Alfred ignored the other Nosoi's comment.

"Oh no wise-guy, you don't get to just go right on to the boss. You've got to go through the three of us first." Deacon explained with a sinister grin from his misshapen mouth.

"Alright then." Al drew his rift blade from his belt and gave a great slash through the spirit's figure.

The Nosoi's image wavered for a moment but then returned to normal. It was clear that Alfred's attack had not inflicted any damage.

"Henry, give them a blast." The resolver commanded.

The wolf brought its head back in a quick howl before bringing it forward with great speed. He unleashed a brilliant beam of golden light from his mouth. The beam tore through all three spirits, but yet again their images returned unharmed a few moments later.

"You can save your fighting for Phthisis. In order to get past you'll have to defeat each one of us individually in a challenge of our choice." Tyraine explained.

"Fine. Name your challenge you grubby spirits." Al folded his arms across his chest with a sigh.

"You'll be facing me first." Alcina spoke up, stepping past her two brothers and standing mere inches from Alfred's face.

The resolver turned his nose up at the smell of her. "How is it I can't slash you bastards but I can smell you. Ugh."

"Don't you want to know what my challenge is, pretty-boy?" she scoffed at him.

"Let's have it then."

She walked a few paces away until she stood before a great barren patch of the cliff. With a clap of her vile green hands the landscape changed. A track had appeared, marked in red pavement and blocked in by rails on either side of it. It turned sharply in some places, circled twice, and appeared to have a variety of objects moving within it. Nearby, two go-carts materialized and roared to life- putting out little wisps of smoke from their tailpipes.

"You're challenging me to a go-cart race?" Alfred exclaimed.

"You're damn right I am *pretty-boy*." Alcina spat back, taking a seat in one of the mini vehicles and indicating for Al to do the same.

With a shrug to Henry, Alfred climbed into the other one.

# CHAPTER FOURTEEN

The entire cavern stretched around fifteen feet from one side to another. The roof, also comprised of the glowing red stone, was at most ten feet tall. Although there was currently a lot going on, Marcie noticed that the portal Alfred went into had sealed itself back up the second he left. Neither of the two rift resolvers with her had access to their weapons, as they lay struggling against the strings that encased them. And of course, there was now the problem of the massive spider that stood before the one tunnel leading out of the cavern. Marcie was trapped.

The thing pointed one of its eight fuzzy[31] legs at her tentatively, eyeing the scimitar in her hand with a few of its eight eyes. She kept all of her focus on the arachnid, watching its alien-like movements and wondering when it would attack. It was velvety black in color, so it stood out against the surrounding red of the cavern. Its back was hardened like the rocks around them and sloped upwards until it came to form a cylindrical shape with an opening at the top. Marcie wasn't exactly sure what this part was for, as the silky webs were coming from its rear. She took the scimitar up in both hands and readied it before her chest.

"Marcie what the hell *is* that thing?" Aaron asked from the ground nearby her.

"That's a spider of some sort, though what kind is beyond me. Never seen a brute that large, nor with a bloody volcano on its back before." Silas answered for her.

"Hurry up and cut us loose, it doesn't seem like it wants to fuck with your sword." Flux urged.

Still keeping her eyes on the spider, she carefully took a step toward Aaron. Immediately the arachnid bunched itself up and the cylinder on its back fired

---

[31] Fuzzy things are not always friendly things.

out a stream of thick red-orange fluid. Marcie dove to the ground, the stream of liquid flying over her. She got to her feet fast and the spider instantly became more wary again.

"It really *is* a volcano on its back. That thing just shot hot magma at you!" Petrou lamented.

"How about I kill the fucking spider first and then cut you guys loose?" Marcie spoke through gritted teeth.

"Yup, that's all good with me. No complaints here. That sound alright to you, Aaron?" Silas inquired.

"Oh ya, totally fine. Kill first, then free- got it." Flux agreed promptly.

Marcie took up her readied stance once more with the scimitar held out in front of her. With great speed she rushed toward the creature. Her head was low but so was her aim. With two quick slashes she dismembered the front two legs of it. It released a sickening shriek-like noise and shifted itself to balance on its remaining limbs. Marcie quickly rolled from out of its reach, but the spider had begun launching an assault of lava from the cylinder on its back.

She raced around the room, jumping here, sliding there- avoiding the streams of molten hot lava whenever they came close. The monster paused its onslaught for a moment, it seemed it wasn't able to keep this kind of attack going nonstop. Marcie was damn near out of breath, but her background as an assassin forced her to utilize her opponent's break. She pushed off from one side of the cave wall, allowing herself to slide on her armored stomach all the way under the arachnid. It noticed her, but had no way of stopping the scimitar from slicing off three more of its spindly legs. Marcie continued her slide all the way through the length of the creature.

"Woo, great move! But hey this lava is getting a little too close for comfort." Flux cheered from the ground.

Marcie got to her feet fast but the spider was well aware of her location now. It sat awkwardly on its three remaining limbs, but managed to shoot a line of strong-as-steel silk that wrapped around the lower portion of her legs. She stumbled and tripped, finding her feet now bound together. Looking up in a panic, she saw the freakish creature crippling its way toward her slowly but with great determination to finish its prey. Her scimitar lay on the ground a few feet away. Unfortunately (for the spider) this assassin's armor was equipped with a few more blades. With a rough movement of her tied legs, something sharp slid out of each piece of armor covering her shins. She gave a great kick and the little knives sliced through the sticky webbing.

She got herself some distance from the crawling thing and popped the two knives out of their places at her shins. She cursed herself for choosing the scimitar as the main weapon her armor concealed, it took up too much room and she preferred to have a better variety of blades on hand. Oh well, she thought, I'll just have to make do with what I have.

"My lady." Petrou's voice interrupted her thoughts for a moment. "I realize you're quite busy at the moment but if you wouldn't mind trying to finish the damned thing, the lava from its back is nearing me and good man Flux here."

Marcie tore her eyes from the spider for a moment to see that Silas was right. The magma that had been shot at her was now oozing gradually closer to where Aaron and Silas were stuck on the floor.

"Right, looks like I need to finish this up then. Just a moment." She told him.

Thinking quickly, the assassin realized she didn't necessarily need a better variety of blades. She did have a few other kinds of weapons concealed in her Altarian Rue armor. She took aim at the spider and threw the daggers into two of its eyes. It lurched and toppled over on its side, unable to maintain balance on what was left of its legs. Now she had her chance. She started up in a great sprint, reaching a hand to the slot on her back that held her store of grenades. Then she allowed herself to drop into a slide on her knees, angled in a circle so that it brought her to the opening on the spider's back. With one well-aimed and well-timed chuck, she hurled the grenade into the volcano on its back.

Breathing hard but knowing she was now running on short time, she managed to pluck a dagger from one of the eyes she had struck a moment before. Now on her feet again, she ran to Aaron and cut him free.

"Rift. Now. Grenade in spider!" Was all she had time to shout at him as she set to work cutting loose Petrou.

Aaron fumbled for his gun, opening a rift beside the three of them. The spider's webbing was strong, and where Marcie had cut somewhat easily through the bit that trapped Flux, she was struggling with the tiny dagger against the thicker webbing around Petrou. Aaron glanced at the spider, it looked to be in great pain and was trying to crawl back down the tunnel it had come from. As he watched Marcie struggle to free Silas he had a terrible thought. The grenade's timer would have enough time for them to get out, but not if the magma inside the monster ate through the shell of the weapon first.

Flux knew he had to take action, he wasn't about to let Marcie or the great Silas Petrou die like this. He grabbed the assassin by the arm and pulled her into the rift beside him. He heard her give a surprised shout, but couldn't make out the words before she was teleported away. Now he bent down, scooping up Petrou with both arms.

"My good man-" the archer said in surprise, but before he could finish Aaron was already leaping through the rift with the man in his arms.

Aaron emerged a moment later on the pebbly underfoot of the terrain outside of the tunnel entrance. He found Marcie's hands steadying him, and he managed to set Petrou down without throwing him. He watched as she finally managed to cut him loose from the webbing.

"That was brilliant, we all might have been spider-food if not for the lady here. And you, Flux, you managed to get us all out before the hulking thing exploded hot magma all over us. I offer my greatest thanks to the both of you."

"Don't mention it." Marcie shot back.

Flux flashed a huge smile; he didn't have the words to express how good the praise from the man made him feel. He turned to Marcie, who was sitting on a boulder and taking stock of what weapons she had left.

"You really were awesome in there Marcie, especially being pregnant and all." he commended her.

"The woman is carrying a child and still managed to put on such a fierce showing! I must say I am tenfold impressed now!" Petrou offered before she could speak.

"Yes *Aaron,* I appreciate it. But remember how you weren't supposed to tell anyone about that? And yet what did you just do?" she watched as the wheels turned slowly in his head.

"*Ooh* right. Sorry about that." He grimaced slightly in embarrassment.

"Your secret's safe with me lass. Congratulations by the way." Silas ensured her.

She gave him an appreciative nod before saying, "So what are we going to do while we wait for Al?"

"Actually, I had an idea about that. And it might even make up for letting slip about the whole prego ordeal." Aaron raised his eyebrows.

"Never say prego again and we can just call it even right now Fluxy." Marcie said but couldn't help giving a laugh.

What could Aaron Flux do for me, she wondered with great curiosity.

# CHAPTER FIFTEEN

The go-cart was easy enough to control, and as Al tested the steering wheel it seemed the whole thing turned with only the slightest touch. He pulled it up beside Alcina's, which was poised just before a line painted on the start of the track. Unsure of how the race was going to begin, he looked over to the spirit.

"Simple, point A to point B. First one to cross the finish line wins. Go when the light turns green." She explained before hacking the nastiest lump of spit onto the side of his cart.

With a slight frown of disgust, Alfred turned back to face the road in front of him. He watched as a pole with a series of four circles rose up from the ground in front of them. The first circle illuminated in red, then the second one flashed yellow. Al revved the cart up a little, still holding in the brake. As the third circle turned yellow as well, he wondered to himself what the consequences of losing might be.

"You've got this sir!" Henry the wolf cheered from where he sat beside the other two Nosoi on the sidelines.

The fourth circle lit up in green. Al lifted his foot from the brake while slamming the gas down harder. His go-cart's back wheels spun with a whir of white smoke as he was propelled forward down the track. It was at this moment he realized he was in no ordinary cart; these things were *quick*.

The first curve to the right was approaching. It wasn't particularly sharp, but Alfred let up on the gas a little as it was his first real turn in the vehicle. It quickly dawned on him that slowing down had been a mistake. He watched as Alcina went drifting around the turn and out in front of him. Coming out of the curve himself, he accelerated the cart fully and took a moment to look at some of the other controls it contained. Ah, there was the lever he was looking for. The e-brake. We'll see who can drift now evil bitch, he thought as he began to slipstream behind her and then come around on the side.

This time it was a sharper turn to the left. Al pulled the lever and got into his drift a second sooner than the female Nosoi. With a thrill he watched his cart straighten out of the turn and come out a few lengths ahead of his opponent. He had forgotten how fun driving something that doesn't fly through space was.

Now came the first obstacle of the route. As Alfred continued to race forward he nearly lost his breath as he saw an old man in the road ahead of him. As he slammed on the brakes, his eyes recognized the man instantly as Papari. Oh no, he thought, I'm not going to be able to stop this thing in time. He closed his eyes as the car skidded through the man and reopened them when he didn't feel any impact. Looking behind him he saw Papari was gone- it had merely been a hologram.

With a sinister laugh, Alcina raced ahead of him. Alfred was angry now; what a devious trick by the dirty spirit. As he got his cart back up to pace, he saw that the track was about to come around left again through a ninety-degree corner. That would bring the road out to where Alfred had walked up the path of torches upon first teleporting there. Of course, there was no path or torches now. The track that formed out of nowhere had replaced them. But an idea popped into his head.

He watched as the Nosoi drifted the super sharp corner with superb skill. Slowing down some, he grabbed his rift blade from his belt and held it out with one hand toward the hood of the little vehicle. The damned thing might not be able to get him off Thear, but so far it hadn't let him down in rifting somewhere on the planet he had already been. He forced the gas pedal completely to the ground and held the wheel straight, even though the corner was now rapidly approaching. Then at the last second, so that he was absolutely flying down the road, he stabbed the tip of the blade into the hood of his cart.

Alfred emerged an instant later with a straight path ahead of him. With a quick glance over his shoulder he saw that he was once again in the lead. Alcina snarled, obviously not happy about his little trick. Well, he thought, if she wants to play dirty so will I. The next curve was a slight right and Alfred drifted it with ease. He gave Henry a wave as he flew by, the wolf cheering him on with a howl. Now they were headed away from the structure at the cliff's edge.

Alcina was still a few cart-lengths behind him when he noticed the next portion of the track. It was quite obviously a ramp, and a very wide and inclined one at that. Alfred couldn't see what it jumped over nor the road on the other side of it. But with rails on either side of him it seemed he had no choice but to jump it. He straightened his cart out on the center of the road. The resolver wanted no interference before he jumped the thing.

His heart skipped a beat as the wheels left the road and he suddenly found himself airborne. Looking over the side of his cart he saw that there was indeed a purpose for the ramp. A chasm filled with bubbling lava was beneath him. Alfred felt the front of the cart begin to dip forward and he had to physically lean back in his seat in order to prevent a nosedive. He blew out a great breath of relief as he touched down on the road again, realizing he had held it in the whole time he was in the air.

Without looking behind him, he knew the spirit had made the jump by the noise of her cart's wheels coming in contact with the red pavement again. He was surprised when he heard her close-by as he went around a left banked curve. Somehow the spirit was gaining on him. Thinking he could use the same tactic again, as the road was coming back toward where they had been before, he steadied his blade in one hand. It looked like there was only a sharp right and a straightaway between him and the finish line.

"Oh no you don't." he heard her voice sneer.

A foul sticky substance wrapped around the blade and it was yanked from his hand. He didn't have to turn his head to watch the Nosoi speed past him with his rift blade. So what, he thought, the spirit had thwarted his attempt. It didn't stop his ability to drive. He brought the hand that had held the weapon back to the wheel as he let it fly around the turn. Alcina's cart was only just in front of him now and all that was left of the race was the straightaway in front of them.

He was gaining on her, but not fast enough to be able to pass before the finish line. Thinking of a different tactic, he came up so that his cart was directly behind hers. So close that the smoke from her muffler was beginning to choke him up. There was only another couple hundred meters to go. Keeping the wheel straight with his knees, Al scrambled out of his leather jacket[32]. His cart was mere inches from the rear end of Alcina's own. He bundled the jacket up quickly and with a well-executed throw, managed to get it between her back-left tire and the wheel casing. He raced past her go-cart that had brutally toppled over and crashed into the guard rail.

Alfred crossed the finish line and with a triumphant shout headed back toward the gate at the cliff's edge. He climbed out of the cart and was met

---

[32] The very same one he's had since Henry first recommended it to him on the Lonely Hearts Intergalactic Cruise. R.I.P.

with an embrace from Henry standing on his furry golden hind legs. The track completely faded into the black ground beneath them, and once more the torch-lit path appeared. Deacon and Tyraine approached him slowly. A moment later Alcina faded into view beside them.

"You play rotten, rift resolver." She glared at him as she spoke, but then her teeth curled into a foul smile as if she commended him for it.

"I figured some road-burn might actually make you look a little better, it's too bad it doesn't affect spirits." Alfred shot back.

"So you've won the first challenge, kudos to you Lýsi. But now you'll have to face me and I'm afraid you won't find this challenge nearly as childish as my sister's little race." It was Deacon who spoke now.

"Why does everyone keep calling me that? My name is Alfred and I know no one by that name." Al questioned, slightly frustrated.

"All in good time. Are you ready for your next challenge, resolver?" the spirit snarled to him through its disfigured lips.

Alfred said nothing, he simply stood waiting for Deacon to explain. If the spirit wasn't going to answer questions, he certainly wasn't about to answer any of his. Especially something so dumb as "are you ready?" As if he had much choice.

Seeing that Moreno had no intentions of answering, the Nosoi spoke up. "I hope you like to swim."

The black field in front of them began to change again, and Alfred had a sinking feeling that things were about to get wet.

# CHAPTER SIXTEEN

"Where are we?" Marcie asked as she exited the rift Flux created into a grand hall with purple columns running along each side.

"We're at the academy." answered Petrou beside them, he seemed to be in a reminiscent state.

Marcie could see through the gaps in the columns; on the right there seemed to be a great body of water, to the left she could make out a mountain range. The floor they walked on was inscribed with strange writings and symbols all the way down. As they got about halfway across the length of the hall, the columns were replaced by solid purple walls and doors began to appear regularly on both sides. They seemed to be headed toward the two stone doors at the end.

"And what are we doing at the academy right *now?* Alfred and Henry could come out of the tunnel at any time and find us *not* there." she directed this question at Flux.

"You'll see, you'll see. As for Al, I left him a note remember?" he reassured her.

The note, secured to a boulder outside of the tunnel entrance, read as follows:

Dear Al,

Had to go off to the academy real quick, I don't think it'll take too long. Boy have you got some surprises waiting for you when you get back! Oops, forget that last part. Anyway, best of luck fighting the evil spirits and all that.

See you soon,

Aaron Flux

"A note you didn't let me read." Was all she responded.

"Ah I wouldn't worry about it Miss. I think you'll be satisfied when you see what we're doing here." Petrou consoled.

They were just coming up on the stone doors when the one on the right swung open. It seemed to open without any great effort or mechanism involved. This appeared normal to Aaron and Silas, though it puzzled Marcie. Now they had a view of the inside. It was nearly impossible to see what the room was for due to the massive line of people and other lifeforms stretching back all the way out the door. This had obviously been the reason for the door opening in the first place, to allow the line to continue on out of the room and down the great hall. Aaron approached the man who had opened it and now stood waiting in line just outside the room.

Marcie noticed two main things about the man. Well, three actually. The first was that he couldn't have been more than five feet tall. Second, he had a rift blade at his belt. And third, perhaps even more significant than his height, was that he had the most awful looking walrus-style mustache that was dyed bright red.

"This is the line to see Arbiter Huro, right?" Aaron had to bend his knees as he spoke to the man.

Now Marcie noticed a fourth thing, the man spoke as if he had just inhaled helium from a balloon.

"Yes, that's right. The Arbiter is quite busy today it seems." Came the nasally response.

Aaron turned back to Marcie and Silas. "Well looks like we'll be doing a little standing. We've probably got some time to kill anyway."

"Aaron, there's got to be at least fifty people in front of us. Is whatever we're doing here really necessary? I don't want Al to think we just left him and I'm worried."

"Oh come on now Marcie. Al knows we'd never just abandon him and besides, your worrying does nothing more on Thear than it does right here." Flux calmed her.

"Well… I suppose you're right." She admitted.

"And Marcel-"

"Aaron do not call me that, I'm already not in the greatest of moods." She glared at him.

"Right, and Marc*ie*, you shouldn't say there's fifty *people* in front of us. Other lifeforms could take great offense to that." Flux lectured.

The assassin merely rolled her eyes.

As if trying to prove his point, Flux got down on his knees and tapped the little man on the shoulder to get his attention.

"Sir, if you don't mind me asking- what species are you? I don't think I've ever met anyone of your kind before."

The red-mustached man became enraged at Aaron's words, getting up in his face and yelling in his high-pitched voice.

"What *species* am I? What *SPECIES?* I'm a human, a *MAN* you nincompoop! And believe me, you ever ask a question so moronic as that again, I'll show you just how man I am." The little man turned away from him when he was finished and Flux got back to his feet.

Marcie looked as if she were about to make a snide remark as Aaron wiped spit from the man's raging speech off his face. Petrou made no attempt at all to hide his laughter.

"Not a word Marcie. Not. A. Word."

**\*\*\* \*\*\* \*\*\***

The range of black land in front of the gate and balcony had transformed into a swimming pool. It was a pool similar to that which one might see at their local intergalactic rec center. The only main difference that Al noticed were the numerous diving boards of various heights lined up along its edge. He turned to Deacon beside him. The spirit had removed all of his clothes, save for a yellow speedo. If Al thought the Nosoi was ugly before, he was now exposed to perhaps the most repulsive thing he had ever laid eyes on.

"So, what exactly is the challenge?" Al asked him.

"Two words for you. Belly. Flop." Deacon rubbed his hands around his greasy boulder of a stomach and laughed as he saw a look of surprise enter the resolver's eyes.

"What kind of operation are you Nosoi running here, anyway? A go-cart race, now a belly-flop competition? What's next, a basketball game with too-tall over there?" Al looked over at Tyraine, who was now wearing a basketball uniform.

"Oh you've got to be kidding me." The resolver put a hand to his face and sighed upon seeing he had guessed correctly about the next challenge.

Deacon seemed a bit taken aback, "And what's wrong with our challenges?"

"It's just, I expected you guys to like, you know…"

Henry finished the thought for him. "He expected you guys to fight him to the death or something similar at least. Instead you've brought before him an array of childish games. It just seems a tad unprofessional is all."

Something peculiar happened then. Alcina came forth from where she was standing beside Tyraine and approached Alfred. He was surprised to see there were tears in her eyes. She placed a green hand on his shoulder, which he instinctively flinched away from.

"What is all this? Another game or something?" he asked the female spirit.

"No… games…" she mumbled between her sobbing.

"Is someone going to explain what's going on here?" the other two Nosoi had now gotten closer to him and seemed to be absorbed in a similar sadness as their sister.

Henry snarled as Tyraine, Deacon, and Alcina all wrapped their arms around the resolver. Alfred started to reach for his blade, but then realized they weren't doing him any harm. In fact, it seemed they were *hugging* him.

"Oh Lýsi, we're so sorry." Alcina wailed.

Al had had enough. He pushed the three Nosoi away from him and moved closer to Henry.

"I'm just about done with all of this. Who is Lýsi and why in Mother's Moons are you all crying?" he demanded.

Deacon came forward again. The swimming pool and diving boards returned once more to the black rock, and a toga reappeared on the spirit in place of his speedo.

"We are sorry Alfred. So truly, terribly sorry. The challenges were just our attempt to delay you from meeting your fate with Phthisis. We… we just didn't want you to die. You're- well you're family." The spirit seemed to be overcome with emotion as he finished his explanation.

Alfred was at a loss for words. Family? With these disastrous beings? And yet he had learned so many strange things about himself during his time on Thear that he couldn't disbelieve it outright. He looked as if he were about to say something but then Alcina started up again.

"You, your real name is Lýsi. And though our Mother denies us, we are her children also. That makes us…" once more the tears came streaming down her green face.

"Brothers." Tyraine finished.

"Y-you know my mother? We're siblings?" Al stuttered.

"Alfred be careful, this seems like a trick." Henry advised.

'Tis no trick golden wolf. We are the Nosoi, born from the goddess Nyx without a father. To be clear, that makes us half-siblings. Lýsi happens to have a father." Deacon explained to the A.I.

If there was any ruse to all of this Alfred suspected it would have come out by now. There were dozens of questions pooling around his mind, but one that seemed more important than all the rest in that moment.

"So, if you're all my kin… what does that make Phthisis?" he finally got the question out, though he feared he knew the answer before it even left his mouth.

A new voice. A timeless voice. A dark, vile, and rotten voice, now echoed from the gate behind them.

"That makes me and you, dear Lýsi, brothers. And no mere half-brethren like the idiots around you. Yes, we share the goddess of the night as our mother, but we also have the same pathetic excuse of a father- Erebus god of darkness. What a pleasure it is to see you again."

And although there was no body associated with the voice that Alfred could see, the iron-wrought gate now swung open. It seemed clear that the time had come for Al to face his past- perhaps the only hope for Thear's future.

# CHAPTER SEVENTEEN

Three hours of standing later and at last Silas, Aaron, and Marcie were at the front of the line. The little man scowled at Aaron as he made his way past them. It seemed to Marcie, in almost all aspects, that this room was meant for some kind of court proceedings. A thin stretch of wood counter separated the rest of the line from those facing the Arbiter. Aaron remained standing, but motioned for Marcie and Silas to take a seat behind a table to the right. The Arbiter sat in the center of the court area on a high seat and was clad in purple robes adorned with similar symbols as those on the floor of the grand hall.

"Alright and what do we have next? State your name and business before the court please." The Arbiter spoke wearily to none of them in particular.

Though one wouldn't consider him to have an old face, the judge did have a good many creases in his forehead and his chin was absorbed in a gray goatee. Aaron seemed to take in a nervous breath before speaking.

"Resolver Aaron Flux, your honor. I am here on the business of invoking a request to have Marcie Devlash be inducted as an official member of the Rift Society."

"What?" Marcie stood up from her seat.

The Arbiter hardly reacted; he was quite tired from the endless stream of cases he had already heard today. When he spoke again it was in the same monotone voice as before.

"I take it the young lady is Miss Devlash? And by her tone, might I also suppose she was not aware of the purpose in her being here today?"

"That is correct." Marcie answered for herself. Adding a moment later, "Your honor."

"Alright, you may be seated Miss Devlash. But before we continue, if we need continue at all, I should ask- is it your wish to join the Society?"

Marcie glared at Aaron for a moment then thought about what the Arbiter had asked her. Join the Society? To her it seemed like she'd already been a part of it for the last few months. And of course Al was dedicated to the Society… as much as she wanted to be mad at Aaron for not telling her or asking her first, she realized she actually did want to join.

"What role would I be coming into exactly, as a member? I have no training with rifts and all that." She asked Arbiter Huro.

"That depends on the case Mr. Flux here has for you. You do wish to proceed, though?" Huro raised an eyebrow at her.

Marcie narrowed her eyes at Aaron once more but finally answered with a simple, "Yes."

"Alright then resolver Flux, the floor is yours." And with that the Arbiter sat back in his chair and folded his arms across his chest.

"Your honor, I am requesting that the lady in question be inducted into the Society as a Drillmaster. Marc- Miss Devlash," Aaron corrected "is highly trained in the arts of hand-to-hand combat, swordsmanship, and stealth."

The Arbiter seemed to be slightly more interested than before, noticing the armor Marcie was equipped in.

"Very well, I suppose all that really stands in the way is the matter of providing evidence of her skills and an endorsement from two current members of the Society. You I take it are one of said endorsements, and this other gentleman is- *Holyfugginspaceballs!* Is that Silas Petrou?" there was no tiredness in the Arbiter's voice as he recognized the resolver beside Marcie. The crowd of people that had built up behind them gasped.

Silas got to his feet, setting his bow and cannister of arrows on the table in front of him before saying, "That is correct, honorable Arbiter Huro."

Most everyone waiting in line to have their cases heard were now arching their necks in an attempt to catch a glimpse of the famous rift resolver.

"My apologies to the audience for my language, but for Chaos' Sake it really is *the* Silas Petrou! I and many other members of the Society were deeply concerned when news came that you were stranded on some backwater planet outside of the Imperium's jurisdiction. I am happy to see you are alive and well!" Huro nodded his head in respect to the resolver once he had finished.

"I thank you for your kind words Arbiter. But I would not be here in your honorable presence today if it had not been for the actions of the lady in question. Miss Devlash single-handedly fought off and killed one of the vilest creatures I've ever seen. It was a colossal spider of sorts, a species that spewed binding silk from its rear and molten lava from a hump on its back. I was caught off guard and found myself trapped in its webbing along with good man Flux here. I assure you that had she not been there, I wouldn't have lived to ever pull back my bowstring again." Silas held Huro's gaze for a moment longer before he sat back down.

"Well you've certainly got two fine endorsements Miss Devlash. The word of these resolvers holds you in high standard. That leaves only the small matter of a demonstration of your skills, and though I suspect you are highly trained, it is simply one of our policies that you provide a showing. Should you be accepted into the Society at the rank of Drillmaster, you'll be in charge of training acolytes of our academy in the arts of combat. So, if you're ready?"

"I'm ready." Marcie swallowed her nerves as she got to her feet.

"Alright then." The Arbiter climbed down from his seat and approached the table by Aaron, Marcie, and Silas. "I will open a rift to the official testing grounds. We will return here upon completion of the trial."

Huro had brought with him a mallet, which Marcie had presumed was only used for purposes of the court. But this mallet was exceptionally large and she watched as the man slammed it into the ground, opening a decent sized rift where it struck. With a nod he jumped down into it. Marcie waited for Aaron and Silas to go first.

"What're you waiting for?" she asked Flux.

"I'm afraid we can't go with you. Just the way these things are lass." Silas explained.

"Good luck, we'll be rooting for you! Here, in the courtroom, where you can't see or hear us!" Flux offered.

Marcie shrugged, thinking to herself it *was* a secret society after all, then jumped in after the Arbiter. She found herself landing on a grassy hillside, with more hills rolling on into the distance. There wasn't a tree or shrub in sight. Looking to the left she saw Huro beside her.

"It's a very straightforward trial Miss Devlash. Do you know where we are?" he asked her, rubbing the end of his scruff with his free hand.

"You can call me Marcie if you like. And no, I've no idea where we are." She responded.

"Okay then Marcie. We are on an incredibly tiny planet known as Ripkin. This planet is the official combat testing grounds for the Society. Ripkin is home to only a single species, but a very curious one at that. The Gigglewarts live to do two things and they seek to do them as quickly as possible. Do you have any guesses what those two things might be?"

"Um… logically speaking, your honor, one of those has to be to mate?"

"Very good! The Gigglewarts seek to reproduce and die. In that order, and that's it. They eat nothing, drink nothing, desire nothing more than to reproduce and then pass on. Well, they do one more thing as well- perhaps the name of the species arouses another guess at what that might be?"

"They um… giggle…sir?"

"Correct again! But they only giggle when they die, as they are so pleased upon receiving death that they just can't help explode in laughter. Sometimes while they *literally* explode." The Arbiter gave a little chuckle to himself as if the thought amused him.

"So, you want me to *kill* them?" Marcie asked cautiously. She was a trained assassin and had absolutely nothing against killing creatures she'd never encountered before. But didn't want to seem too eager for bloodshed to the man in charge of whether or not she got into the Society.

"My, you're a marvelous guesser! Yes, kill as many as you possibly can actually. There's no time limit, you simply go on killing the damned things until you're absolutely too exhausted to continue. At that point, you'll have to make your way back here and press this red button." As if his words had been some sort of trigger, a small pedestal rose up from the ground. A large red button sat on its top.

"Can I ask a question?" she inquired.

"Of course."

"Do the Giggle, um Gigglewarts, attack back?" she asked somewhat awkwardly.

"Quite the contrary really, though I think you'll find they can become quite a nuisance as their number grows. Anyway, I can't tell you how many need to be done away with- only that there *is* a certain quota that must be reached. Therefor you should really keep killing until you're completely wiped out. Well, not literally, you still have to make it back to the red button once you call it quits. Upon finishing we will return to the courtroom to view your results."

"Alright, I'm ready. Oh wait, I didn't get a chance to restock my weapons." She noticed, suddenly more worried.

"Oh good, that reminds me! I would've completely forgotten and then we'd have had to start this ordeal all over again. There're no weapons allowed and I'll need you to remove your armor."

Now that came as a surprise. Marcie hadn't fought anyone or any*thing* without her armor in years. And without any weapons she'd be forced to combat them all with only her fighting skills. Oh well she thought, a little practice without the armor could do me some good. She pushed the armor in a variety of places and it popped off with a whoosh of pressure releasing. She wore only a tight pair of black leggings and a green tank top underneath. Worst of all, she had no shoes, for her boots had been part of the armor. With some regret she handed the pieces over to Huro. The man slammed his mallet into the ground once more, presumably opening another rift back to the courtroom.

"Alright, simply hit the red button when you're ready to begin, then hit it again when you're done. Best of luck!" and without giving her a chance to ask any more questions, he hopped into the rift and was gone.

"Alright Al, I'm doing this for me, you, and-" she looked at her stomach for a minute, "and our future. So you stay safe and kick some evil spirit ass and I'll wipe the hillsides with these Gigglewarts."

And with that she slammed her hand down on the red button.

# CHAPTER EIGHTEEN

Alfred started walking toward the opened gate. He halted for a moment before he took the first step past the boundary it marked.

"Coming Henry?" he called behind him.

The golden wolf bounded toward his friend, but just as he made to leap across the invisible line he was sent violently flying back. Henry let out a yelp.

"Henry! Are you alright?" concern for the A.I. flashed across his face momentarily, but Henry had gotten himself back on his paws.

"Something is preventing me from entering sir." The wolf explained.

"The gate marks a barrier." Alcina began, "It is infused with godly powers and can only be entered by the true children of Erebus and Nyx. Not even we can enter."

"Alright then Henry, looks like this one's a solo mission." Al patted the wolf on its head. "You should head back and find the others anyway."

"Yes sir…but are you sure you'll be alright?" the A.I. tilted his head.

"I'll be fine, don't sweat it." Alfred made as if to step through gate but was stopped short once again as Tyraine called out.

"Brother wait, you have no idea the power of Phthisis and how badly he wishes to destroy you."

"Hey now look the three of you, if you really are all my family then I'm not just going to sit around and watch our older brother bully you into doing his dirty work. This Phthisis sounds like a real jerk and I'm going to teach him a lesson or two about family."

"Is there anything we can do to help you Lýsi?" Deacon offered.

"Yes, as a matter of fact, the three of you could do me a great help by leading Henry out of here and back to my friends."

Alfred nearly fell over as the three Nosoi swallowed him up in yet another hug. The stench was overwhelming.

"Alright, alright that's enough of that." He managed to break free from their grasp. "Phthisis hasn't said anything since he opened the gate and I don't like that. Get Henry out of here safe and back to my friends. I'm counting on the three of you."

The three Nosoi backed off and raised a salute to Alfred, saying in unison, "We won't let you down Lýsi!"

With one last nod to Henry, Alfred turned around and stepped across the boundary of the iron-wrought gate. Nothing seemed to change other than the outline of a path on the ground was now visible and when he turned around the gate was closed with none of the others in sight.

"Looks like there's no going back now. Not that I planned on it anyway." Al grinned to himself.

He walked forward for a minute or two longer, the path before him illuminated only by the eerie light that seemed to be resonating from whatever lay over the edge of the cliff he was now approaching. He stopped a foot short of the edge and peered down below. Beneath the cliff was a massive swirling lake of violet light. It certainly didn't appear to be any sort of liquid, but Al had seen stranger things than a lake comprised of light.

For the second time the bodyless voice rang out. It seemed it could have been blasting out from across the entire lake or just directly into Alfred's mind.

"Go ahead and dive in, if you really wish to face me. The *great Lýsi* isn't scared of heights, is he?"

Alfred didn't say a word. The one speaking to him might technically be his brother, but he would never recognize someone so vile as his kin. This was the one responsible for all the devastation on Thear. The one who was causing needless suffering on this ancient planet- the planet Gaea told him was the origin of all humanity. He was the one who was forcing the Nosoi to do his evil biddings. So Al felt no reason to reply to Phthisis' childish gibe and with eyes wide open and arms spread out, he stepped over the edge of the cliff and fell down, down, down.

Though he didn't expect to feel any sort of real impact, as the rift resolver fell through the lake of light he did feel something shift. It wasn't a sensation of feeling as much as it was just being in a different place. A *very* different place. The violet seemed to be all around him now. Billowing up in cloudlike formations here, simply radiating bright waves of color everywhere else. At some point Alfred allowed his eyes to close, becoming used to the sensation of falling through the light. His eyes could have been closed an instant or an hour, but he opened them when he felt his feet land softly on ground.

Though he had jumped from the cliff edge spread-eagle, he was now standing upright inside some kind of structure. The light had become the ground he now stood on and this was all that illuminated the vast building. The ceiling appeared to stretch on forever and the whole place was of a cylindrical shape. The room was empty except for a small glass enclosure in the center. The shape of the glass resembled an oblong egg and though the floor's lighting was dim across the whole room, Alfred quickly realized it wasn't empty. There was an extraordinarily beautiful girl inside. She was pounding against the glass, but no sound came to Al's ears. He rushed up to face her. Upon reaching the enclosure he immediately recognized Gaea.

"I'll get you out goddess, I promise." Alfred spoke for the first time in the strange place.

It was impossible to tell whether the goddess had understood, but she stopped banging on the glass for a moment and stared into the resolver's eyes.

"That's quite a bold promise. Do you really think you can keep it?" the voice of Phthisis was instantly recognizable, however now it seemed as if it were coming from much closer than before.

"Show yourself coward. You're going to release her *now*." Al called out to the opposite side of the room.

At last he stepped forward and the voice of Phthisis was finally associated with a body. This spirit was not dressed in a toga as the Nosoi had been. He wore a black tunic with a matching cloak draped around his shoulders. As he strolled around the side of the glass enclosure Alfred saw that he was quite tall, or was at least giving that illusion. The eyes of Phthisis were green, but not the lustrous welcoming green that Alfred saw in Gaea. These were a horrid, hazy green, filled with all the infection, rot, and disease that embodied the spirit himself.

As Phthisis came to stand in front of him, Alfred was surprised to see that the spirit's hair was white, though he had the face of a man only a little older than himself.

"Release her? Release her, you say? Now why would I let such a beautiful goddess go when she's just about done with the process?" Phthisis stroked his chin, mockingly considering Al's request.

"What process, what are you talking about?" Alfred demanded. Though he was a good bit shorter than the spirit he faced him boldly.

"Take a closer look, brother." Alfred put his face against the glass and peered inside.

155

The resolver could see Gaea laying in the middle of it, her eyes now closed. But as he looked closer, Al could see a strange green haze slowly approaching where she lay from all around. Angrier than ever, Al tore his gaze from the goddess of Thear and directed his attention on the daemon once more.

"*What* are you doing to her?" he insisted.

"Why I'm merely preparing her, dear Lýsi. Once the process is complete and the Haze of Spoil has overcome her entirely, I'll not only have a new bride but I'll also be ruler of Thear. Which of course allows me to spread forth a hell of a lot more destruction and decay into the Universe than I've ever been able to before."

"I'll never let you get away with this." Having had enough, Alfred slashed his rift blade up and into the direction of Phthisis' chest in a heartbeat.

"You'll need to be a bit quicker than that. My, it *is* fun rough-housing with your little brother. Go on, let us waste more time as the haze overtakes my new queen." Phthisis was now standing three feet behind Alfred, the resolver's blow had completely missed.

He's just stalling, I've got to get that case open before it's too late, Alfred thought. Turning around he saw Phthisis raise an eyebrow.

"Go on, strike again. I'm *sure* you'll get me this time." he sneered.

"You got it." Alfred threw his left arm forward as if he were attacking the spirit, but chucked his rift blade behind him with the other arm directly into the glass cage.

With hope he turned around. Only to see the blade strike the glass and fall to the floor, the enclosure still intact. This seemed to have awoken Gaea in the center again and she looked as if she was trying to say something.

"A lovely little trick, but I'm afraid no silly rift blade is going to break through that." Alfred still had not turned around, trying desperately to read the goddess' lips.

Al said nothing as Phthisis went on, "You've always been the favored one. Out of all of us, not just you and I. Mother and Father were so proud and sad to see you go the day you were chosen to leave the heavens. I was there that day, I watched in disgust from the far edge of their realm. So pleased Erebus and Nyx were to have born a child meant to do good in the Universe, not the destruction most of their other children have brought forth."

It looked as if the first word Gaea was saying was Lýsi. Lýsi, Al thought, that's what everyone here keeps calling me. He almost had the second word down now- meat? Mean? No, he realized, she's saying *means. Lýsi means...*

"But no more. Mother and Father will have to accept me once they see the great power I have amassed! Who would ever have thought that I, Phthisis, would defeat the goddess of Thear and conquer her world with darkness and decay?" the spirit appeared to be talking more to himself than anyone else at this point, but Al had heard enough.

"Will you *Shut Up!* I'm sick of hearing about your stupid plan, I'm sick of not knowing who I am, and I'm *sick* of everyone calling me Lýsi when I have no clue what it means. *Ugh!*"

There was a newfound rage inside Alfred now, a level of anger he had never encountered before. He could feel it pulsing through his body, growing in his gut, and flashing in his eyes. He looked away from Gaea for a moment, seeing the Haze of Spoil was about to overtake her. When Phthisis noticed him, the spirit's face lit up in shock.

"Y-your eyes…they're glowing. What is-"

"I've had enough of not knowing. It's time I found out a few things." Alfred's voice sounded an octave deeper now and resonated with power.

The resolver turned back to the glass case, not even picking up his blade from the ground beside him. He placed both hands on the glass and began to force all of the rage and anger he now possessed into breaking the cage. Phthisis appeared beside him, but before the spirit could do anything Alfred turned his burning gaze on his brother once more. The light from Al's eyes seemed to scorch the evil soul, and Phthisis stumbled backward clutching his face and wailing in pain.

Alfred focused back on Gaea's message, staring at her lips as she mouthed out the words and he tried with all his will to break the glass.

"Lýsi means… Lýsi means… Lýsi means *WHAT!*" suddenly the same golden hued light that was in his eyes began to burst out of Alfred's palms and into the glass.

Phthisis' cry was lost in the sound of the enclosure finally breaking, the fragments of glass shattering onto the violet floor of light. Now Alfred had no need to read the goddess' lips. He could hear every word she said clearly.

"Lýsi means the solution. *You are the solution.*"

# CHAPTER NINETEEN

At first Marcie thought something had gone wrong. She pressed the button as the Arbiter instructed and yet nothing had happened yet. She stood on the hillside looking out across the land, keeping her eyes peeled for any sign of life. Then she saw it. Just coming over one of the distant hills, Marcie could barely make out a line of something approaching.

"At this rate they won't reach me for another half hour. What a bore." She groaned to herself.

*Tap.*

Marcie spun around fast as she felt the gentle hit on the back of her leg. Standing at knee-height was a creature directly behind her! And she hadn't even heard it approach! It was about two feet tall, covered in a wooly pelt and had the biggest, most adorable eyes Marcie had ever seen. The Gigglewart looked up at her and promptly wrapped its tiny arms around her leg in what could not be described as anything other than a hug.

"Uh, hey there little guy." Marcie reached a hand down and picked the creature up by the wool on its head.

The Gigglewart did nothing more than continue to stare into her eyes with its adoring look. It seemed to have no concern nor feel any pain at being lifted by the fur on its head.

"Well fella, real sorry about this but it seems you must be one of those giggle things. I don't know how you managed to creep up without me hearing, but regardless one fact remains true. You've gotta die."

And with that Marcie tossed the little creature into the air and met it with a swift kick that sent the Gigglewart flying down the hill. The assassin looked down to where the body landed. The eyes, though now bruised and bloody, were still looking at her in adoration. Marcie jumped back when it made a noise.

"Hehehehehe!" and then poof, the Gigglewart disappeared in a small puff of smoke.

"Well that was easy. And disturbing, mostly

disturbing. These little things don't even try to fight back."

*Tap. Tap.*

The assassin whirled around once more as she felt a tap on each leg. Now there were two more of the Gigglewarts touching her and she hadn't heard them approach either.

"Where in the hell are you guys coming from?" she directed the question at the creatures but was really asking herself.

Suddenly both of them clasped their tiny arms around each of her legs. Marcie, never one to be fond of touching, promptly picked one up in each hand as she had with the first one. Then, trying hard to ignore their innocent gazes, slammed the Gigglewarts together hard. They disappeared in a puff of smoke and cry of laughter once again.

"Well, there's three already. I can't say they're much of opponents, but they are quite stealthy."

Looking out over the land it appeared the line of Gigglewarts she had seen initially were still far off.

"I've never been a fan of people, or anything for that matter, sneaking up on me. So I think I'll just go out there and meet those little bastards." Marcie took off running across the hills, kicking stray Gigglewarts each time she encountered them.

**\*\*\* \*\*\* \*\*\***

For a moment the golden light faded from Alfred's hands, though the gleam of it still resonated in his eyes. He quickly put himself between Gaea and Phthisis, who seemed to have gathered himself. The daemon of rot took a few steps toward them as he spoke.

"Here we go again with this ridiculous prophecy. *Oh behold the great Lýsi, the solution for Thear and all that goes wrong in the Universe.* Pure garbage, that's what that is." Phthisis mocked.

Now Gaea spoke from where she stood behind Alfred. "Well it seems to me he's already proved you wrong."

"He's proven *nothing*. Will mommy and daddy's little chosen one take me on? Or is he too *scared?*" the spirit sneered.

"Listen here Phthisis. I've never known our mother and father. I've only just learned the true meaning of my name. But what I do know for sure, is that you're way out of line and I intend on putting you right back in your place."

"Alfred wait, you must be careful! I have no way of helping you here. My powers are centered around flourishing life and all that remains here is death and decay."

"Right. Don't worry about me right now Gaea, I'm going to teach this jackass a lesson."

"That's an awful lot of talk little brother. Let's see what you've got to back it up." Phthisis rushed toward him with a sinister laugh.

Alfred knew he couldn't simply dodge the attack, doing so would put Gaea in danger behind him. His opponent was smart, he'd give him that much at least. And on top of that, Al had no real idea of what these newfound powers were, nor how to use them effectively.

Looks like my best bet is the old-fashioned route, he thought to himself. Alfred ran and snatched his rift blade from the ground, throwing it immediately toward Phthisis. The blade missed, but the resolver's intent was not to inflict any damage. A rift had opened in the gap between the daemon and the goddess. The evil spirit went directly into the portal and appeared a moment later right in front of where Al now stood.

As Phthisis' face came through the other end of the rift Alfred met it hard with his right fist. But he gasped as his hand went right through the spirit.

His brother gave a sinister smile, "Nice trick, but I'm afraid punches of that caliber won't work on me. Haven't you realized that yet?"

Alfred's eyes opened wide in surprise as he felt the spirit punch him painfully hard in the gut. A small spatter of blood escaped the resolver's mouth as the breath was knocked out of him and he fell backwards.

"Lýsi no!" Al could hear Gaea's shout.

Al could see Phthisis approaching him fast, but his thoughts were focused on what his brother had said when he punched him. *"Punches of that caliber won't work on me."* I get it, Alfred thought. But his thinking had left him vulnerable and distracted, and before he could move out of the way he was sent reeling from another punch to the jaw.

"The solution huh? What a joke. It was nice to see you again brother, but I'm afraid I have planets to conquer and you're wasting my time." Alfred looked up to see Phthisis standing over him.

The daemon extended both arms and clasped his hands together, raising them into the air ready to bring down the final blow. But Al had learned the trick now. Just as a resolver combines their energy into the Universe's and directs it into a blade, Alfred found he could direct this new godly power into whatever part of his body he chose. It took intense focus, especially since he had only become aware of this ability minutes before. That's why he let his brother hit him the second time, he'd been focusing only on sending the golden light into the soles of his feet.

"How about kicks of this caliber instead?" Alfred shouted as Phthisis swung down his double hammer-fist.

Al kicked both legs up from where he lay so that they made contact with the daemon's interlocked arms. Phthisis released an eerie wail of pain as the godly power infused into the resolver's double kick sent the spirit's arms flying off his body. But Alfred wasted no time now, he got to his feet and sprinted to where his rift blade had stuck in the ground.

Then, with incredible speed he rushed to stand behind his brother who was kneeling on the ground, staring at where his arms had been a moment before. The daemon tilted his head back to look Alfred in the eyes. Eyes that burned with the divine light of godly power.

"Brother please, spare me. I see that I have done wrong and I wish to make amends." The spirit begged.

Alfred's eyes softened for a moment, as the pleading reached his ears.

"No Lýsi, do not trust him!" Gaea shouted.

But her warning came a second too late. Phthisis slammed his head back into Alfred's groin, causing the resolver to fall over in a gasp of pain. In an instant the daemon was back on top of him, his foot against Al's throat.

"An excellent attempt, but not good enough." The spirit snarled.

"I-I agree. You t-tried hard Phthisis, but you'll never b-beat me." Alfred choked out through the pressure on his throat.

In the next few seconds a lot happened. Alfred had his rift blade held between his two feet, and while his brother had been talking he managed to transfer the godly power into the blade itself. The knife now radiated with a brilliant amber glow. Al brought both legs upward and sent the blade deep into the center of his brother's spine.

The pressure on his throat alleviated as Phthisis' eyes went all white and he toppled over onto the ground. Now Al stood above him one last time, pulling his blade out of his back and rolling him over on his stomach.

"I know little of my family and even less of my past. But I will *always* fight for what is just and right." The godly light faded from his weapon and eyes as he went on. "Still, I'm ashamed that I was forced to kill you brother. I wish I could have made you see the light[33]."

"You did what had to be done Lýsi. You have saved Thear, the planet once known as Earth and the origin of all humanity- the very planet I embody. For this I am forever thankful to you." Gaea walked over and put a gentle hand on the resolver's shoulder.

---

[33] His spine sure saw the light. Too soon? Nah

"I guess." Alfred's head was still down and he watched as the body of his brother faded away until nothing remained on the ground beside him.

"I have not forgotten my promise to you, nor to your parents." Gaea continued and Al looked up at her now as she spoke. "I will take you to meet them now. If you so wish."

"Right." Alfred pulled himself together a little and nodded to Mother Earth. "I'm ready to meet my parents."

# CHAPTER TWENTY

That's probably enough, thought Marcie, as she felt a few beads of sweat trickle down her forehead. The assassin forced her way through the endless masses of Gigglewarts that had come to surround her. A kick here, a punch there, a couple headbutts and at last she slammed her hand down on the red button. Almost immediately the creatures stopped their efforts in grabbing and touching her and began to head out in all directions toward the distant hills. With a sigh of exhaustion, Marcie sat down on the grass.

Not a minute later a rift portal appeared and out dropped Arbiter Huro. He seemed confused as he looked around him, until his eyes found Marcie and he offered her a hand up.

"Hello Ms. Devlash, how do you think you did?" he asked with a smile.

"Judging by the smile on your face, I'd say I did pretty good." Marcie replied confidently.

"Oh no, I'm simply being friendly. Haha! We won't know the results until we return."

Marcie looked slightly embarrassed at her comment, but before she could say anything the Arbiter spoke again.

"This smoke that seems to have taken precedence over the air is quite puzzling to me. Do you have any idea where it might be coming from? This planet is not meant to have any outside influences and if there's a problem I'll need to get the maintenance team here to check it out."

Marcie looked above her, sure enough there was a smog that had filled the air around them.

"Oh, well that's from the Gigglewarts your honor. I'm certain you know they turn into a puff of smoke when they're killed?" she explained.

The look of surprise was unmistakable on Huro's face. "You mean to say that you killed… oh never mind, we'll find out when we return. Shall we?"

Marcie nodded and the Arbiter proceeded to open a rift for each of them to walk through. An instant later she was standing beside Silas and Aaron again and Huro was back in his chair.

"The required tally is five hundred Gigglewarts for anyone in the Society who will have the responsibility of training others in combat. Most give up when the masses of creatures begin to overwhelm them. We will now see the official Gigglewart count of Marcie Devlash." The Arbiter announced.

A screen above him that had been blank now came to life. It read:

Required tally: 500

Official tally of Marcie Devlash: 5357

Congratulations, you have set the new record.

Previous record: 1020

Aaron's jaw dropped. Silas took a nervous step away from Marcie with a respectful nod. The Arbiter smiled again.

"Welcome to the Rift Society, Drillmaster Devlash." Huro announced.

The people and lifeforms still waiting in line broke out in applause. Marcie smiled as she lay a gentle hand on her stomach.

*** *** ***

"Now that you're aware of your godly powers, you could open a rift to the gods' realms with your blade. But since you haven't been to Erebus and Nyx' domain before, I will show you the way this time."

Gaea looked directly at Alfred; her eyes illuminated in a bright flash of green that sent the comforting feeling coursing through him once more.

Al felt like he had simply blinked from the brightness of her eyes, but he now found himself somewhere new. The dim lighting was similar to where he had fought Phthisis, but the darkness here seemed different in a way he couldn't put into words. He saw Gaea in her white dress walking in front of him and he began to follow. Alfred wasn't sure how long they traveled through the darkness- the sensation of time seemed to be almost nonexistent here.

Eventually they came to a fence line and followed it to the right for a while. At last Gaea stopped; in front of her was a grand gate carved from obsidian. The darkness around them seemed to make it shimmer in a way that yet again Al could not comprehend. The goddess of Thear stepped aside and motioned for Al to approach.

"It would be rude of me to enter first, as this is not my domain. I think you'll come to find that gods and goddesses are very particular when it comes to mannerisms such as this."

"Alright, if you say so." He replied, stepping up to the double-gate and pushing it so that it swung open wide.

He took a few steps inside then turned to make sure Gaea was following. The beautiful goddess was right behind him. A powerful voice interrupted his pace. A voice that sounded as dark as the ever-night around them.

"Who dares enter this province without my permission? State your name and business or be tossed over the edge of eternal darkness." A man stepped out from the shadows in front of Alfred.

He wore a navy suit with a matching cape that dragged along the ground behind him. He had jet black hair combed neatly back and a matching goatee was squared around his mouth. His eyes were the blackest pits of darkness Al had ever seen. The resolver turned to Gaea for a moment, who nodded with encouragement.

Al forced himself to look the man in the face and taking a deep breath before he spoke announced, "My name is Alfr- well I guess my name-"

"What is this Gaea? Some sort of jest? A man who isn't even sure of his own name? Leave now before I call for my wife." Erebus interrupted.

Gaea looked as if she were about to explain, but Al spoke boldly before she could. "My name is Lýsi, and I have come to see my parents. Speak to the goddess like that again and we're going to have a problem."

Erebus seemed taken aback. For a moment the god was speechless, but then he uttered a single word, "Lýsi."

"Yeah that's right, now apologi-" Alfred was interrupted once more, but this time it was from the man wrapping his arms around him.

At first he thought it some form of attack, but the man's grip was nowhere near threatening. A second later it dawned on him, this guy was hugging[34] him too!

"Uh…" Al shot Gaea a questionable glance.

"Lýsi, this is your father. Erebus, the god of darkness." She explained.

"My… father?"

The god unwrapped his arms from Alfred and wiped what appeared to be black tears from his cheeks.

"I'm sorry for how I greeted the two of you, I had no idea at first. But the way you stood up to me, the god of darkness, you've got to be my son! Anyone else would have surely pissed themselves by now!"

"Well if that's the case, I'm glad to meet you Erebus." Alfred couldn't help but crack a smile, this was his real father after all.

---

[34] Who would have thought a sci-fi action/adventure would have so much hugging? I did, that's who.

"Come, your mother will be thrilled!" Erebus grabbed one of Al's hands and began to lead him away.

"Wait, what about Gaea?" he managed to stop, though it took a lot more strength than he liked to admit.

The goddess answered for herself, "I think I'll be heading back to Thear now. There is much to revive and replenish now that the evil has been eradicated. Thank you again Lýsi, you will always be welcome on my planet."

And with that, Mother Earth placed a kiss on Alfred's forehead and took a few steps back toward the obsidian gate. A bear materialized beside her, and she climbed on its back before it pounded away into the darkness.

"Ready then son?"

"Right, let's go!" Alfred couldn't help but let the excitement come through his voice, he was about to meet his real mother.

They walked on for a while longer until they came near an overhang. Alfred noticed a bench sitting right on the edge- there was a woman on it. Al looked expectantly to Erebus, who confirmed his suspicion.

"Oh Nyx my dear, look who's come to visit at long last."

The woman on the bench vanished and reappeared a second later in front of Alfred. She was tall, almost taller than Erebus himself. Her eyes were black like his father's but Al thought he could see tiny flecks of silver within them. Her long black hair seemed to be made of shadow itself. She wore a beautiful dress that flowed all the way to the floor, where it seemed to somehow combine with the darkness there so that one could not see her feet.

First she looked into Alfred's eyes, and he couldn't help but get the chills a little. Next she pulled on one of his cheeks and he tried not to flinch. Then, walking around him once, she finally returned to stand in front.

"Um hel-" Al attempted to start the conversation.

"Have you been eating enough? You're so thin, you've hardly got any meat on those bones!" Nyx interrupted.

"Umm… well I-"

"Oh I'm just kidding! Isn't that what mothers are supposed to say?" And she wrapped him up in her arms so tightly that Alfred thought he might freeze to death from the chills she was giving him.

This went on for another minute or two, until at last Nyx released her son. Then the three of them sat down at a small table that materialized out of the darkness. Here they sat for a very long time, and

Alfred enlightened them with what life had been like for him so far below the heavens. Eventually he came to tell them the story of his mission to save another resolver on Thear and how he was forced to face Phthisis. When he got to the part where he freed Gaea and then had to kill his brother, he got very solemn and expected his parents to be even more upset.

"I'm so sorry, I had no choice. I just... I had no choice." Was all he could manage to get out.

Both his father and mother put a hand on him then, and looking back up he saw no disapproval in their eyes. It was Erebus who spoke first.

"Phthisis has long envied you Lýsi. He witnessed Chaos choose you as the solution and this angered him. Long after you were sent below the heavens, he too went down in a fit of rage and must have went to Thear. Although we are no pictures of goodness ourselves, we have always longed for our children to follow their paths. Phthisis chose his and you were chosen for yours. What happened, happened[35]."

---

[35] Although it might seem a tad cruel, the fact that Erebus doesn't seem very concerned with the death of his son is actually quite commonplace among gods and goddesses. Sure, they mourn the children they lose, but siblings and other family members killing one another is more common than one would like to think in the godly realms. Therefor, unless a child of a god is particularly significant to them (take Alfred for example) they likely will mourn the loss and then simply make more. There are, of course, cases where the parents choose to exact revenge- but that's a different tale for a different day.

"Your father is right. It's a shame what was forced to happen between the two of you. But we do understand. We will mourn the loss of Phthisis, our son, even though he acted out of jealousy and rage." Nyx agreed.

Alfred was able to breathe a little easier after hearing his parents' take on what happened. They sat around together for a little longer and the god and goddess showed Alfred around their realm. Eventually Alfred began to think of Marcie and figured he should get back to her before she was overcome with worry. His parents were sad to say farewell, but knew the obligations their son had to the worlds below the heavens. Alfred infused his godly light into his blade and sliced open a rift near the obsidian gate. Then he turned and hugged each one of them.

"Oh there's one more thing I'd like to ask of you Nyx, if you don't mind."

"Anything my son."

Alfred approached his mother once more and whispered in her ear. A look of surprise came over her face for a moment, but then her gaze softened.

"Yes, they are welcome here. I'll take care of it." came her reply.

Erebus shot his wife an inquisitive look but seemed unconcerned at whatever had passed between her and their son.

"Well so long, I'll be back to visit before too long. Goodbye mom, goodbye dad."

"Take care son!" Erebus called.

"Make sure you get enough to eat! And remember you're always welcome here!" Nyx reminded him.

And with one last look at his true parents, Alfred stepped through the golden rift.

# CHAPTER TWENTY-ONE

"Alfred!" a cheery robotic voice was the first thing the resolver heard as he exited the golden rift and found himself outside the entrance to the tunnel.

"Henry, hey buddy! Glad to see you made it out alright!" Al greeted the egg as it helicoptered up to meet him at eye level.

"We ran into a couple obstacles, but thanks to these three I made it out just fine." The A.I. indicated to the Nosoi with a flash of light.

"Henry saved us a couple times too." Alcina admitted.

"So Lýsi, if you're back does that mean Phthisis is… dead?" Tyraine asked.

Alfred then explained what happened after he entered the iron-wrought gate. He didn't really expect the Nosoi to be saddened by the death of their half-brother, but he was a bit surprised when they all cheered "Hooray!" upon hearing the news. I suppose he was always a bully to them, Al thought.

"Well you guys, what do you suppose we do now?" Deacon asked the other two.

Neither Alcina nor Tyraine seemed to have an answer. Then Alfred spoke up.

"Oh yeah, I almost forgot! I talked to our mom-"

"*You talked to our mom?!*" they exclaimed.

Alfred laughed, "Yes, I talked to Nyx and she says the three of you are welcome to the domain of darkness and night whenever you please. I think she had some explaining to do to Erebus, but I'm confident you three will be welcomed there by now."

"Brother… how can we thank you? You've saved us from Phthisis and provided us with a place to call home." Alcina seemed to be on the verge of tears.

"No more crying you three." Alfred started, "You can thank me by listening to Nyx and Erebus. Make yourselves useful to them in any way you can."

"We won't let you down Lýsi!" Deacon shouted with joy.

"Let's go right away! I wanna see our new crib!" Tyraine announced and then vanished with a wave to Al.

"Come visit us soon brother." Alcina added and then her and Deacon vanished as well.

"I think you're a pretty great brother for not knowing you had any siblings just a little while ago." Henry commented.

Alfred seemed to be absorbed in reading a note that was taped to a nearby boulder.

"Oh yeah that's from Aar-" Henry was interrupted by a flash of purple light beside them.

Suddenly Aaron and Marcie appeared. Alfred immediately caught her in an embrace and they kissed for a moment before Aaron spoke.

"Hey Moreno! Did ya take care of those nasty spirits or whatever?"

Alfred rolled his eyes to Marcie, "Yeah Flux, I took care of it."

"Hey guess what!" Marcie shouted all of the sudden.

"Marcie's an official member of the Society now! She even set the new record[36] for-"

*WHACK*

Aaron slumped to the floor, completely out cold from the smack of Marcie's armor against his face.

Alfred stopped his laughter and turned back to Marcie, "You're really in the Society now?"

"Well yeah, it was kind of Aaron and Silas' doing but it was still my choice to make." She explained.

Marcie looked into Al's eyes, trying hard to read his reaction. But it was obvious when he spoke, "That's awesome honey! And you set the record for most Gigglewarts killed I'm guessing?"

"Sure did." She gave him a wink.

"That's my little assassin. What happened to Petrou?"

"Oh, he got assigned a new mission while we were at the academy but he told me to tell you thanks again for everything. And by the way, it's *Drillmaster* Devlash now."

Henry joined the conversation, "So Drillmaster Devlash, are you going to tell Alfred the *other* surprise?"

If looks could kill an artificial intelligence, Henry surely would have dropped dead right then.

---

[36] The previous record for Gigglewarts eliminated was held by none other than Overseer Bradley Martin.

"What other surprise?" Al was puzzled at the sudden tension between the egg and his girlfriend.

"Nothing that can't wait a little while longer. I think one surprise a day is enough. *Anyway*, you're the one that has some story-telling to do. Tell us about what happened!"

"Ugh, babe I know you want to hear about it, but I've already told the story twice in the last couple hours. And I had a little surprise myself, but you're right- one a day is probably enough." Alfred smirked.

"Oh come on!" she complained.

"I'll fill you in on the way to where we're going next, but I *guess* I can tell you the surprise now. Only it's just I sort of messed up a big part of it already…" he offered.

"Messed it up? Just tell me Al!"

"Wait, hold on a second- I have an idea! Henry come over here." The A.I. followed him over behind a boulder where Marcie couldn't see.

"Hey Henry" he whispered, "Remember that ring I had to give to Old Red?"

"Oh yes sir, I see where this is going! You can count on me! I'll use a little of the crystal's power for a temporary transformation." the little egg answered excitedly.

When Alfred came back around the boulder a few minutes later Henry was nowhere in sight.

"Hey where'd-" Marcie started.

The assassin went silent as she watched Alfred get down on one knee.

"Marcie Devlash, I love you with all my heart and soul. I've traveled across countless galaxies but in all my time as a resolver- no, in all my life- I've never seen something as beautiful as you."

Marcie appeared to be speechless and tears could be seen brimming in the corners of her eyes. Alfred pulled out a small golden ring from his pocket.

"And more than that, I've never experienced anything that makes me as happy as when I look into those emerald eyes."

"Oh, Alfred…"

"This was gonna be a lot cooler right now because I had an emerald ring and I thought the line I just said would have went really-"

Suddenly the gold ring spoke up from Alfred's hand, "Oh just ask her already, sir!"

Alfred grinned. His robotic friend was right.

"Marcie, will you marry me?"

Fewer than a handful of times had Marcie Devlash cried in her life, but now she didn't even try to stop the tears streaming down her face.

At last she managed the answer, "Yes."

Alfred slid Henry the ring onto her finger and they laughed as he cheered in excitement before they shared a kiss.

"I love you." She said softly.

"I love you Marcie." He returned.

"So where are we headed next sir?" Henry chirped, bringing the sentimental moment to a close.

"I was thinking a little vacation would be good for all of us, whaddya say?"

"With all five of us, sir?" Henry buzzed.

"Henry there's only fou-"

"Henry if you don't shut up right now I'm going to throw this ring back down the tunnel."

"Oh enough fighting the two of you. Come on, let's get off this damn planet already."

"Marcie I hate to have to leave your finger already but I believe Mr. Flux is going to need my assistance. I promise I'll go right back to ring-form when we get to wherever Alfred has chosen!"

"It's fine Henry." She replied, pulling off the ring that transformed back into an egg a moment later.

Al pulled his blade from his belt and sliced open two rifts. Then, taking Marcie's hand in his, they walked through the first and it closed behind them. Henry extended out his hook and attached it to the collar of Aaron's shirt. He then proceeded to drag him through the other rift.

"Come on sir Flux, we're going on a vacation!" the A.I.'s words rang out cheerfully as they crossed through the portal and finally left the planet Thear behind.

# ABOUT THE AUTHOR

Mason J. Schneider was born in the city of Des Moines, Iowa. However, his family moved around a bit and he was raised in a small town in Ohio. Here he has had the odd summer job and also worked as a cashier in the local grocery store. He lives there to this day with his cats SneeSnaw and KinKoo. (Yes, they have very strange names.)

Mason's imagination led to him writing *The Wizard of the Night*, a children's fantasy series, and his young adult (he emphasizes adult for this series) sci-fi *Al Moreno Rift Resolver*. He plans to continue to write adventurous tales for as long as he can.

In his spare time Mason enjoys hiking, reading, writing poems, watching movies, and having good times with friends. Growing up his father built a library inside their house, so there was never a shortage of books and this is likely where his love for reading began. In the future Mason hopes to be able to use his writing to help others around the world.

Oh, and he also paid someone to write most of this author bio. Because while he might be confident in his book-writing abilities, he admits he is quite lackluster when it comes to talking about himself. And also finds it really weird referring to himself in third person.

Website - www.riftresolver.com
Twitter - @mayso35

Made in the USA
Monee, IL
31 August 2023

41936113R00114